Team Destiny and Patty's Probation

Belinda White

CHAPTER 1

If anyone had told me I'd be helping Ruby bring in a bond runner on my wedding day, I'd have outright laughed in their face. And yet, here I was, ready to do just that.

For the record, it had taken a lot of convincing on Ruby's part to get me here. Part of that was the whole wedding day thing, but another part was the fact that I'd never been all that fond of caves.

That's right, caves. Holes in the ground big enough to get lost in. Or worse, trapped in.

This wasn't even one of the larger cave systems with guided tours and all the safety items that went along with that, either. Nope. I couldn't get that lucky. A public cave wouldn't be all that great of a place to hide out, now would it? But a private cave was a different matter.

Especially for an outdoor survivalist geek like Morgan Lee.

This had been a hard nut to crack for Ruby. I was proud of her for really digging in her heels to solve the riddle of where Morgan had literally gone to ground. Looking around, I was pretty sure she was spot on, too. It was just too perfect for that not to be the case.

I took a deep breath and turned from the mouth of the cave to look at Ruby. "I need to call Trevor before we go in."

She tilted her head. "You know he won't approve of this, what with the fact of the wedding tonight and all." She paused. "Is this your way of backing out?"

"No. A promise is a promise, and I said I'd help you." I glanced back at that dark opening. "I just want to talk to him before we go in. If he tries to call while we're in there, he could get worried."

Ruby didn't look so sure, and she had the right not to be. If there was any way for me to get out of this and still save face, I would. I really, really didn't like caves.

Truthfully? It surprised me that Ruby was up for this. Of course, without me there beside her, she probably wouldn't be. She was counting on my power to get us both out alive if we ran into trouble.

That wasn't all that comforting of a thought to me. A dead witch has no power.

I took a few steps away and dialed Trevor. He answered on the first ring.

"Hey, babe. You miss me yet?"

"It's only been one night, you know. And keeping the tradition of the groom not seeing the bride on their wedding day before the ceremony was your idea, not mine."

He chuckled. "Hey, I know it's just a superstition, but why take the chance? We need all the good luck we can get, and none of the bad kind."

I had to agree with him there. For a few seconds, I debated telling him exactly where I was and what I was about to do. But Ruby was right, he would probably have issues with this, so if I was going to keep my promise to Ruby and not tick off my very soon-to-be husband, then I should probably just keep my trap shut.

"You should know I'm helping Ruby out this morning."

There was a few seconds' pause. "Anything dangerous?"

Boy, how did I answer that one? "Um, no, the person she's after is Morgan Lee. She got her tracked down, but she just needs someone to help, that's all."

"Morgan Lee? Isn't she the activist that ruined all that equipment from the lumberjacks' camp?"

Yeah. Pouring sugar into gas tanks worked pretty well at stopping the big machines. "That's her. She has a history of property damage, but nothing to show that she has a violent nature. We should be fine." My eyes went back to that dark opening, and I swallowed. I really hoped I was telling him the truth with that last part.

"Okay then."

Something in his voice told me that something was on his mind. My witch's intuition kicked in. "You sound a bit distracted, Trevor. You aren't having second thoughts, are you?"

"About tonight? Heavens no. If there is one thing in the world I'm certain of, it's that I want to marry you tonight under that blessed full moon."

"Then what is bugging you? Is everything okay at home? What are you not telling me?"

He blew out a breath. "That darn intuition of yours. Okay, I'll tell you. I'm fine, the house is fine, and Destiny is fine. The trouble is with Patty. She arrested one of the commissioner's daughters yesterday and now the man has called for a special commissioners' meeting to try to strip her of her badge. If he succeeds, they'll likely be expecting me to take it back on again."

"You think he has a chance of getting the votes to do that?"

"He only needs one more. And, of course, he isn't using the arrest of his daughter as the cause. He's focusing on the leave she took to help the council... calling it a dereliction of duty."

I thought I was starting to see the problem. "When is the meeting?"

"A week from Tuesday."

Crapsnackles. I'd been right. We weren't leaving for our honeymoon for another week. That meant that we'd be gone when the meeting happened. Something the commissioner in question just might have had in mind when he scheduled the darn thing. The county thought a lot of Trevor and his dad. Having him speak on Patty's behalf would not help his case.

"You know we can postpone the honeymoon, right?" I said.

"You'd really be okay with that?"

"Of course, I would. This is for Patty. She'd do the same for either of us, and you know it."

"Okay, but we still have a few days before we have to decide for sure. Maybe things will settle down before then and we can unruffle enough feathers to bypass this."

It was a nice thought, but probably not likely to happen. "It's Commissioner Parsons, isn't it?"

"Got it in one. You know his daughters have always been a handful. Making that arrest might not have been the best thing for Patty to do career-wise, but it was one hundred percent the right move to make. Those girls need to realize they aren't above the law just because of who their dad is."

"All right then. We have a plan." I glanced back at Ruby. I could tell she was ready to get the show on the road already. "Look, I'd probably better go and help Ruby with this thing. Don't want to run too late."

"Amie?"

"Yeah, Trevor?"

"Be there tonight, okay? I don't care if you're covered in soap bubbles or soaking wet from a dip in the river. Just be there."

I swallowed. "Goddess willing, I'll be there. I love you, Trevor."

"Love you too. Now go help Ruby so you can get ready. It's kind of a big night, you know." Then he hung up.

Leaving me with nothing other to do than the one thing I most didn't want to do. Go into that cave.

When I stepped up beside Ruby again, she was studying a small, hand-drawn map.

"Is that the layout of the cave?"

She nodded. "Yes. At least as close as Morgan's father knows. He really wants her to come back, stand trial, and get this behind her. And as he's the one that discovered this cave on his uncle's property, well, he knows it better than anyone."

I arched an eyebrow at her. She backtracked.

"Okay, so maybe Morgan has spent a lot of time down there, too. But it looks like a fairly simple cave." Her fingers traced along the map. "Here's the main entrance where we are. Once inside, there's a good-sized cavern and then two branches off from that. The branch off to the left leads to a smaller exit from the cave. The one to the right dead ends."

"And you're afraid that if you go the wrong way, she'll hear you and make it out past you without you knowing it."

"Yup. That's why I needed a backup."

I ran a hand through my hair. "You know, we could have used a third person to stand by that other entrance. Just in case there are more tunnels that we don't know about."

Ruby chewed her lip for a second. "That would have been nice, but everyone is... well, kind of occupied today. And Morgan's dad had the feeling that Morgan was planning something big. He's really afraid she's going to get herself into even more trouble than she's already in."

Ah, that made sense. I'd been kind of wondering why he was being so helpful with the capture of his daughter. So far, none of her protests had resulted in anyone getting hurt. If that changed, then the charges against her would greatly increase in severity. A good father wouldn't want that to happen.

"So, what's the plan?" I asked.

Ruby grinned at me. "You take one path, and I'll take the other."

Fair enough.

I had to choose the path to the right. I'd had a fifty-fifty chance at this, and I blew it. The right path, as it turned out, was the wrong path. For me, at least.

The cave's tunnels weren't all that big. So it was single file walking at the very best. With a lot of twisting and ducking involved the further you got in. Luckily, I wasn't all that far in when I saw her.

Or more to the point, she saw me. Hindsight is twenty-twenty, but I guess I should have dug a little more into who Morgan Lee was before starting this endeavor. Come to find out, she was a teenager. A very small-boned and nimble teenager, at that. That small-boned thing turned out to be a very important and need-to-know fact.

Why? Because old man Lee's map of the cave was wrong. The right-hand branch of the tunnel didn't dead end. There was a much smaller tunnel off to the left that led to another exit. At least, it was an exit for a young girl as small as Morgan. It didn't turn out to be an exit for me. Which was kind of a problem.

I sucked in a breath and yelled, hoping that Ruby could hear me. With my current situation, half in and half out of the cave, I wasn't all that sure she would.

"Third entrance. She's out of the cave, Ruby. Close to the car. Grab her!"

I heard sounds behind me. That had to be Ruby. "You can't get out this way. Go out the front!"

The sounds retreated, and even as I watched, Morgan unearthed a bike from a pile of tree limbs, grinned back at me, and took off riding.

Seconds later, Ruby burst into view, looking around. Morgan had already headed down the dirt path towards the road.

"She had a bike. She's heading for the road," I called out.

Ruby glanced around, probably trying to figure out where I was. And why, if I could see her, I hadn't stopped her. Luckily, to my point of view, my head and shoulders were covered by a blanket of very tall grass. Which happened to be tickling my nose to no end.

She gave up after a second and took off down the path. As long as she reached the end before Morgan got away, she could follow her in the car. But she had to be fast enough to see which way she went.

All that to say, it was going to be a while before help came back for me. Truthfully, I was kind of glad. I really didn't want anyone to see me in this situation. Not even Ruby.

The more I squirmed and wriggled, the more stuck I got. If I didn't know better, I'd swear that exit hole was actually getting smaller by the second. How long before it would cut off my air supply?

Okay, so that probably wasn't going to happen, but still, I wasn't exactly thinking rationally.

Which is why I did what I did next.

Chapter 2

I wasn't quite myself by the time Ruby made it back. That was why I had to forgive her for rushing past me and back into that cave.

A quick glance into the backseat of the car showed me that at least Ruby had her runner. Small win at this point, but a win.

I could hear Ruby calling my name inside the cave. All I could do was hope that she wouldn't try to squeeze out that right tunnel exit looking for me. Ruby wasn't any smaller than I was. And it sure as heck wouldn't help our situation if she got into the same mess as me.

When she returned, I was standing right at the mouth of that right-hand tunnel. She couldn't very well miss me now, could she?

She spared me a quick glance and then, Goddess help me, she stepped right over me, heading for the cave's entrance.

"MEOW!"

Ruby stopped dead in her tracks. In slow motion, she turned to face me. In any other situation, her expression might have been seen as comical. Right now, however, I thought the rather horrified look was more than appropriate.

She swallowed, staring at me for another few seconds. Finally, she whispered, "Amie?"

I flipped my new tail high into the air and meowed again. Cats have such limited vocabularies that speech wasn't really on my side at the moment.

Ruby closed her eyes, then opened them again. I raised a paw to wave at her. Hopefully, she could translate that to... 'yup, it's me, now get me out of this.' That was definitely what I was trying to convey.

The anxiety attack I'd suffered when I got stuck in that stupid exit to this stupid cave, coupled with my stupid pride, had caused me to make a tremendously stupid mistake.

Oh, the transformation spell had worked like a charm. I was living proof of that fact. Unfortunately, it wasn't until after I cast it that I realized I'd only learned half the spell. The part that did the initial transformation. As it turned out, I didn't have a clue how to turn back into my previous self.

Hopefully, Arc could help with that, as he was the master at turning into a cat and back again. After all, that's how the two of us had met. But first, I had to convince Ruby who I was and have her take me to him so he could tell me the second part of the spell.

Sometime before this evening would be nice. Or instead of walking down the aisle with me and Dad, Arc would be carrying me instead. And I'm really not sure the officiator of the wedding would take a meow as an I do.

Not to mention the fact that while Trevor might be okay with soap bubbles and water, I had a funny feeling that even he would draw the line at fur.

Why, oh why, did this have to happen today of all days?

I couldn't really blame Ruby for doing another full sweep of the entire cave, including the area immediately outside it. If I hadn't, in fact, been the cat now sitting on the hood of her car, then she would have to explain to Trevor why she'd left me behind on my wedding day.

So, nope, no blame here. But I sure as heck wished she'd done it a lot faster. This fur was kind of itchy. Soft on the outside, yes, but itchy on the inside. I wanted my nice, smooth skin back. And I wanted it now.

When she finally made it back to the car, she stared at me for a few more seconds. After glancing into the car to make sure Morgan hadn't escaped, which would have been a real trick as she was currently handcuffed to the 'oh, crap' bar and the child lock on the back door was on, she turned back to me.

"If you really are Amie, then wag your tail and meow twice. No more and no less."

I took a deep breath. If that was what it took to convince her, so be it. My tail swished in the air as I meowed twice. Looking her full in the eyes the whole time.

She opened her mouth—probably to ask for even more as-surance of the actual situation—but I'd had enough. I raised up full length to place my front paws on her chest. A real stretch for a cat, even on the hood of the car.

"MEOW!"

Ruby swallowed, shut her mouth, and nodded. "Okay then. Let's get you to Arc."

Finally.

She opened the car door, and I hopped into the front seat. Naturally, she took the wheel. What choice did we have there? I couldn't very well operate the foot pedals and still see out the front window, now could I?

"Cute kitty," Morgan said from the back. "You know, if you're the kind who saves lost cats, maybe you should be on my side. I do what I do for the greater good, you know."

Ruby glanced in the rearview mirror at her but didn't say a word. She had other things to worry about. Namely getting me back into skin form before Trevor found out what had happened.

We might all be able to laugh about this later, but right now, it was most definitely not a laughing matter. Trevor would not be amused at all. He'd only asked one thing of me. Be at the hilltop by the full moon so we could be married.

It shouldn't have been that hard of a request. Now, it seemed almost unsurmountable. I really hoped I could get the message through to Arc that I needed the last half of that spell. If I could just get him to read it to me, I'd be golden.

I could cast the dang thing, change back, and still have time to do my hair and get ready for the wedding. By this time, I was going to be cutting it far too close.

Ruby called Arc on the way and told him to be at the estate when we got there. Then she called Patty and told her the same thing. She couldn't tell either of them what was really going on because of the two ears in the back. No sense in having the entire town laughing at us.

Patty's presence wasn't so much needed for my situation as it was for the situation currently still running her mouth in the backseat. If I'd been in my regular state, I'd have been very tempted to cast a silence spell. Ruby, apparently, was far too distracted by other things to really let the chatter register.

I wish I could say the same. It was just another small thing ratcheting up my worry and stress. Finally, I jumped into the backseat and put a paw on her leg, looking up at her with beseeching eyes.

She looked down at me and shut up. Then she did something I should have expected but hadn't. Morgan petted me. And... it felt nice.

Knowing what I knew now, Destiny would definitely get a lot more petting from me.

Arc is so my brother. Well, half-brother technically, but still. The man didn't take long to get on board with exactly what had happened.

I saw his calculating eyes looking at Morgan Lee and then at Ruby. Most likely noting the size difference between the two. Ruby is about my size. It would be hard for him to compare my actual size to Morgan with me in my current state. With Ruby there, he didn't have to.

While I appreciated the fact that hopefully, all that meant was that I'd have a quick and easy reversal to the spell, I totally could have done without his huge, all-knowing grin. That grin irked me to no end.

Like he hadn't made mistakes of his own by changing into cat form. I mean, come on, he'd been made a bloody familiar. How many witches can say they'd seen life from that end of things?

Once Ruby handed Morgan off to Patty and they drove off to the jail, Arc turned to me. "Let me guess. There was a tiny exit hole that Morgan could get through and you couldn't, right?"

Immediately, the frown that had been so prevalent on Ruby's brow lifted as she looked down at me. "So that's what happened!"

Yeah, yeah, I'd made a dumb mistake. Now get me out of this, guys! Or, in other words... "MEOW!"

Arc laughed. "I'm going to go out on a limb here and say that you only took the time to learn the first part of the spell? Didn't look far enough into it to discover that there was a second, very important piece to it?"

Seriously, if there was a single other person I could turn to for help—and I had the means to get to them by myself—I would have stalked off. He wasn't making this easy on me at all.

I'd meowed all I was going to meow. So I just went with a glare. Then, just for good measure and to be sure my point got across, I lifted a single paw and extended my claws.

My hope had been that would stop the laughter, but it didn't. Nope, now even Ruby joined in. Apparently, a scary as all get out light witch wasn't so scary as a kitty cat.

"All right, all right," Arc finally said once the laughter died down. Then he told me the part of the spell I'd been missing. I filed it away in my head, then stalked off to my own house. Trevor's car was gone, so I should be safe from the whole groom seeing the bride thing. Besides, I could use a little alone time at the moment.

If only that could be.

Arc and Ruby had laughed, sure. But not nearly as hard and as long as Destiny did. It didn't end when I changed back into skin, either.

"It might behoove you to remember your source for crispy-fried bacon," I told her. Then I walked by her, up the stairs, and through my bedroom into the master bath.

One look at the mirror and I grimaced. So much for my shaving routine that morning. That would all have to be done again. Although at least for once, the hair I was shaving wasn't all bristly. It was actually soft and supple.

Not that I was planning to keep it. Nope. Hair under the arms and on the legs just had to go. No matter how soft it was.

After the shower and shave, I relented and let Ruby in the house. Mom's wedding dress—which was very important to me to be wearing down that aisle—was a two-person job getting into. Plus, I was never much good at doing my hair up into elaborate styles.

Hairdos were much more of a Ruby thing than a me kind of thing.

Of course, it would have helped me tremendously if she hadn't been grinning the entire time. I was never, ever, going to live this down. From here until eternity, instead of seeing me as a badass light witch, at least a part of Arc and Ruby would see me as a tiny little kitty cat who had tried to intimidate them with teeny-tiny little claws.

What had I been thinking? Oh yeah. I hadn't been thinking. That's what had gotten me into that mess to begin with.

Nothing to do now but move past it. It was hard, but that was the plan.

CHAPTER 3

We made it to the wedding, with me in skin form and all fancied up as the day required, with time to spare.

And can I just say, wow? The Moms had done a splendid job of decorating that hilltop. Opal and Mom's wedding up here had been gorgeous, but it had to have a tent because of the weather. The Goddess had seen fit to allow my wedding night to be absolutely perfect.

At least, weather-wise. The full moon was just starting its ascent into the heavens. The trees were all still fully leaved. And a light breeze flowed across the hilltop, rustling leaves and cooling the night off to that perfect temperature.

I fully acknowledge that perhaps that perfect temperature had a bit of help from all the witches in attendance, but I still think the Goddess had a small hand in it, too. She had long ago given her blessings to this marriage. That meant a lot.

Mom and Aunt Opal fussed over me for several minutes before the music started. Then they hurried off to their seats as I took my place at the head of the aisle. An aisle strewn with delicate white daisy petals.

My dream wedding in all its glory was laid out before me. Family, good friends, and the perfect man waiting for me at the end of a short, flower-filled walk. No matter what I'd gone through to get here to this moment in time, it had all been worth it.

Then I caught a glimpse of Trevor standing by the altar, all decked out in his wedding tux, and I almost started hyperventilating. How lucky could a girl get to be marrying not only the absolute most handsome man in the entire world but her best friend too?

Dad, to my left, must have noticed my breathing change. "Deep breath, girl. You can do this."

It was a nice sentiment, but it didn't really help. Arc, however, on my right side, took a different approach. "Just think about the expression on his face when he hears about your day."

My feet stumbled just a tad bit on the next step to music, but I recovered quickly. Yup. Those words did the trick, all right. Part of me wanted to glare at him, but deep inside, I knew the words had come from love. And I appreciated them.

The rest of the wedding was just as perfect. The vows were beautiful, and yes, Trevor managed to make me cry. But for the record, I made him cry too. Not a lot, but there were definitely tears in the man's eyes.

After the I do's, we all settled down for a late-night feast and wedding reception. Trevor and I had stressed that we didn't want wedding gifts, but of course, no one had listened.

We made a good haul.

Then, finally, after all the pomp and glory that was my wedding, Trevor and I walked down the path toward the farmhouse with good friends and family lining the way. I'd never felt so loved in my life.

That feeling continued all the way home, and afterward. Part of that is because when we got home, Trevor didn't stop with carrying me across the threshold. Nope. He carried me all the way up the stairs and down the hall to the bedroom, too.

And can I just say right now that I've totally changed my tune about marriage really only being a piece of paper? It's so much more than that.

For the record, you might not think it, but there are definitely perks to sleeping with your husband rather than your fiancé. Even if they were the same person.

Ask me how I know.

Sunlight streaming through the bedroom window woke me up the next morning. Well, that and the somewhat less exhilarating feeling of being watched.

I turned in bed to find Trevor propped up on his elbow, just quietly watching me. When he saw I was awake, he smiled at me. "Good morning, wife."

I grinned back at him. "Good morning, husband."

The possibility of a glorious twenty days together stretched out in front of us, and it felt good. Trevor had cashed in his built-up personal days, and I had cleared my schedule too. This time was going to be all about us.

I, for one, was loving that thought.

Then, with a slight glance behind him toward the bathroom door, Trevor said, "I do have one tiny little question, though."

Basking in love and sunlight, I shrugged. Normally, those kinds of statements filled me with dread. They rarely ended well. But today? I had that feeling that nothing could bring me down from the heaven I was in.

It made me brave. "Shoot," I told him.

"Why is there cat hair on my razor?"

Oh yeah, that. I took a deep breath and told him. Everything. From the trip in the cave with Ruby, to getting stuck in that oh-so-stupid exit hole, and all the chaos that ensued afterward. It felt good getting it off my chest.

No way was something that big going to go undiscovered by my ace-detective deputy sheriff of a husband. In the end, I was really glad that I'd been the one to tell him the story.

It helped me in another way, too. By the time I was done—and yeah, maybe I exaggerated the craziness a touch— Trevor wasn't the only one busting a gut. I was laughing too.

Right up until Trevor's phone rang. He glanced at it, then looked at me with a raised eyebrow.

I shook my head. "Your call, but you might at least want to see who it is first."

He grabbed the phone to look. I didn't like the sudden frown on his face. "It's Patty," he said. Then he answered the call. No way would we not answer a call from her. Even the morning after our wedding.

For what it's worth, Patty didn't believe in rambling on with small talk. "Is Amie there with you?"

"Yes."

"Put the call on speaker, would you?"

Trevor did, then asked. "What's up, Patty?"

For a few seconds, there was nothing more than silence. Finally, she said, "I debated for a full hour before making this call, just so you know. I really didn't want to. But I need you two as I've never needed you before."

"What's going on?" I asked.

"There's been a murder." She paused. "A rather spectacular one that I don't want to go into details on over the phone." Another pause. "I know it's asking a lot. If you say no, there will be no hard feelings on my part. But if you two could spare the time, I could really, really use you here right now."

Trevor's eyes met mine. It wasn't so unusual for Patty to call and ask for Trevor's help. After all, he was her second in command at the sheriff's station. But for her to include me was very unusual, indeed.

This did not bode well.

"Where's here?" Trevor asked.

"Too close for comfort from home, I'm afraid. The park behind our estate. I can have a deputy waiting for you at the parking lot if the two of you are up for this."

I could hear the hope in her voice. She knew she was asking a lot, and if she still asked even knowing that, then there was no way in heck we were turning her down. Not in a million years, should we live so long.

"Give us fifteen," I said.

Trevor hung up, and I made for the bathroom as Trevor started getting dressed. Obviously, he'd been awake long enough to take care of the preliminary essentials. I hadn't.

After taking care of those, I threw on a pair of jeans and a t-shirt, and the two of us started toward the door.

Trevor's phone vibrated. It was a text from Patty. "Have Amie bring her camera. She needs to be seen as a professional on this one."

I ran into my office and grabbed my camera bag, then met Trevor at the car. He'd already pulled it around the front for me. The man didn't let grass grow under his feet when a friend needed help.

This wasn't a matter of a sheriff calling in a deputy. This was a matter of Patty calling in Team Destiny.

I could feel that in my very bones.

Chapter 4

Deputy Wallace met us just as Patty had promised. The fact that he looked more than a little green didn't escape my notice, either. Nor did it bode well for what we were walking into.

We could have questioned him about what was going on, but why make the man talk when we could just walk a little way and see for ourselves?

My first glance at the crime scene had my blood freezing in my veins. At the very least, it felt like it did, anyway.

All those old, horrible movies about witches where they were evil and sacrificed people on huge stone altars under the light of the full moon? Well, the scene in front of me could have been taken right from the center of any of them.

Complete with the dead man on the altar and the witch's athame sticking out of his chest. This was so not good. But it was about to get even worse.

Trevor, like me, stopped dead in his tracks, his hand going to rub down his face as Patty crossed the small clearing over to us. He looked at her. "Please tell me that isn't..." He just couldn't seem to bring himself to say the words.

Unfortunately, Patty could. "Commissioner Parsons." She took a deep breath. "It's him, all right."

Then she nodded to me. "Thanks for bringing your camera," she said in a little louder voice. Those were words for everyone to hear. "I want a full photographic record of this scene. Hopefully, something will show up in it later."

I knew her words were mostly for show. She wanted me here as a witch backup, much more than as a photographer. But that didn't stop the words from being true. Pictures of a crime scene were never a bad thing. And my equipment beat the cell phone images the deputies were taking hands down.

Even as I walked away from them, I was already shooting images. The first priority was to get photos of the body itself. The coroner would likely be here any minute, and I'd never have another shot at capturing a pristine crime scene.

As I snapped the photos, I could hear Trevor and Patty talking behind me.

"Um, Patty, not that I'm questioning this or anything, but why are you here?"

Funny, but it took Trevor's question to make me remember that this area wasn't in Patty's jurisdiction as sheriff. I paused for a second to hear her answer.

"Sheriff Michaels is on his way, but he was out of town when the report came in, so he called me." I glanced back in time to see her grimace. "If he'd known what this scene looked like, I don't think he would have made that call."

I swallowed. As much as I hated to admit it, I thought she was probably right. Not only did Patty and the not-so-good Commissioner have a stormy past, the witch's sacrifice scene before us and the close proximity to our very homes just sealed that deal.

It looked very much like someone was trying to frame Sheriff Patty Bluespring for the murder of Commissioner Parsons. Unfortunately, they'd done a bang-up job of setting the scene. In a very memorable and theatrical way.

We'd have our work cut out for us to disprove that theory. And the only way to do that was to catch the real killer. And fast.

I went back to snapping pictures with a new-found passion. This might be the closest we'd get to this crime scene in the near future, and I wanted the best record of it that we could get.

Unfortunately, I had a very bad feeling we were going to need it.

I wasn't wrong about that, either.

I'd barely managed to make one sweep of the clearing—and trust me, I was shooting images just as fast as my little finger would go—when Sheriff Michaels arrived. He took one look at the crime scene and then sent the three of us packing.

The man even tried to confiscate my camera. Like I was going to give that up without a fight. He rethought himself when he remembered who Trevor was. Trevor was one of Patty's deputies, yes, but the man was also the son of retired sheriff Orville Taylor. He'd even held that title himself for a short spell.

The Taylor name meant a lot in the circle of sheriffs. I had no problem handing over the memory card I'd been using. Not after I'd made sure to copy all the images on it to the camera itself beforehand.

Patty followed us back to the estate in her vehicle, but she didn't take the turnoff that led closer to her little A-frame home. Instead, she followed us straight to the main house. I was glad of that because it saved Trevor and me from having to make the trip to her house.

I made a pot of coffee and poured us each a huge mug of the stuff before any of us said a word. Sometimes coffee and a little thinking time were required before words happened, and this was one of those times.

But once we were all settled at the big kitchen table, Patty ran a hand through her hair. "I've made a real mess of this."

I looked at Trevor and then back at her. "Your phone will show a record that Sheriff Michaels called you in, won't it?"

She nodded. "Yeah, but that doesn't help the fact that I was there."

I frowned. I still wasn't getting it.

Trevor took a sip of his coffee and then took pity on me. "With the look of that crime scene and the fact that Patty and Parsons had some pretty heated words in the last few days, it looks to me like someone is pointing the finger at her."

"With you on that one," I said. "Especially as the crime took place literally walking distance from here. But I still don't get why Patty being there—in her capacity as sheriff, no less—could mess things up."

Patty took a deep breath. "Me being there compromised the crime scene. If any evidence points to me... well, yeah, I was right there, so it would have to be thrown out. But even more important..." Her words trailed off, and she just shook her head.

"More importantly," Trevor picked up, "Any evidence they find now that doesn't have Patty stamped all over it could be said to have been planted by her, as now everyone will have proof that she was, indeed, there."

Crapsnackles. They were right.

"Come on," I said. "Surely people aren't that stupid in this town. If Patty were going to kill the man, that's the very last way in the world she would have done it. She'd have dragged that body so far away from here, and hidden it so well, that it might never have been found. Not put it in what amounts to her own backyard and in plain sight. It wasn't even buried. Whoever did this meant for Parsons to be found. And more importantly, to be found like that. Which anyone in their right mind should know would instantly clear Patty."

Now they were both looking at me.

"You know, she has a point," Trevor said slowly. "You don't exactly have a reputation for being foolish, Patty."

"Agreed. But I don't think it will be that easy to undo the damage. Not with how some people around here feel about witches to begin with." She took another sip of her coffee. "Even when I'm cleared of any wrongdoing in this, the doubt will remain in a lot of people's minds." She looked over at Trevor. "I'm thinking my days as sheriff of Wind's Crossing are numbered. And maybe that isn't a bad thing."

"Aren't you happy with the job?" I asked. I mean, she'd certainly seemed to grow into the position well. Sure, it had been rocky at first, but once she learned the ropes, well, there just wasn't any stopping her. In time, she'd have rivaled my father-in-law as the sheriff of the century for sure.

She shrugged. "I've grown to like it, yes. But a sheriff has to have the backing of the people they serve. I think I might have lost that with Parsons' murder."

"Don't give up on the position too soon," Trevor said slowly. "And please don't go and do anything rash like hand in your resignation or anything like that. All we have to do is prove without a shadow of a doubt that you had nothing to do with this."

I brightened. "Wait a minute. With all that setup, the murder probably happened under the light of the full moon, right? That's what the coroner's report will show. I bet you."

Trevor started smiling. "And we have a lot of witnesses that know exactly where Patty was while that moon shined so bright. If that murder happened before midnight, you have at least a couple dozen reliable alibies on your side."

I nodded. "And not all witches, either. Orville was sitting at your table for the dinner, wasn't he?"

It can't exactly be said that Patty brightened up all that much, but at least she looked a little more hopeful about the situation. I'd take that.

Too bad that little bit of brightness didn't last all that long. Her eyes dimmed a little as she shook her head. "I'm pretty sure we're going to be out of the coroner's report loop. They aren't going to let me near this case now with a ten-foot pole."

Trevor opened his mouth, and Patty and I just looked at him. Eventually, he closed it. Momentarily, anyway.

"I'm going to be out of that loop now, too, aren't I?" He paused. "What with me being married to a witch now and all?"

Patty hesitated. "It goes further than that, too, Trevor. Whether or not you know it, the entire station is abuzz with the gossip about you deciding to become a witch. I don't know who you shared that little tidbit with, but whoever it was, they didn't keep it to themselves."

"Ah, crapsnackles," I said. I meant it with all my heart, too. With the way some people thought about us witches, they'd probably be thinking that Parsons had been sacrificed as some kind of initiation ceremony or something.

This was going to get ugly fast. If we didn't put a lid on this, and soon, it would create a wall between the community of witches and the regular people on the street. A wall that we had spent literally centuries knocking down to begin with.

Patty stood and stretched. "Well, I think we've done as much damage on this as we can for now. The investigation isn't up to us at this point. I just hope the ones in charge can see through the obvious setup. In the meantime, until I'm relieved of my duties, I have a night shift to get to tonight, and some sleep to get before that happens."

I walked her to the door. There was one more little detail I wanted to get out of the way. Because I'd be buggered if I was going to bow out of this one. I was pretty sure that Trevor felt the same way, too.

"Hey, Patty? You know I'm a private investigator, right? You give me the nod, and maybe a quarter as due consideration and retaining fee, and I'd have the right to look into this."

She looked at me for a long minute before digging a quarter out of her pocket and handing it to me.

"Consider yourself hired."

All right. Now we were talking. And I had a lot of work to do to get up to speed on Commissioner Parsons.

CHAPTER 5

Trevor and I spent the rest of the afternoon and evening digging up as much dirt on Commissioner Parsons as we could. I had to admit that wasn't such a hard task. But it was a lengthy one. The next morning, we were still at it.

Truthfully, I didn't understand how the man kept getting himself elected by the people. From everything I was seeing, the man was a bit of a slimeball. He had a long history of breaking campaign promises. And some of those promises were to some pretty influential people, too.

Definitely a place to look into. But why would an influential person or business owner want to frame Patty for the murder? Or make it such a spectacular affair?

That part of it made little sense. This felt more like the culprit would have to have had a beef with both Parsons and Patty. Unfortunately, so far I'd come up blank on that theory.

I looked over the table at Trevor. Normally, I worked up in my office slash library. But that seemed rude as we were working this one together, so we'd both settled with our computers at the dining room table. Plenty of room for both of us to spread out there.

"You got anything yet?"

He shook his head. "Nothing that looks like it could lead to murder. But then again, Parsons wasn't such a nice guy, was he? A lot of people kill for the little things, don't they?"

"Any newspaper will tell you that's true. But the whole sacrifice thing pointing to Patty... that really throws a wrench in things, doesn't it?"

"You can say that again." He paused to rub the back of his neck. "Any chance at all that it wasn't Patty they were trying to point the finger at? Could there be another area witch with a grudge against the man?"

Hm. Hadn't thought about that. "Nothing that I've found so far. But I can check with the local coven here in Oak Hill, to be sure."

Trevor stared at me for a minute. "For the record, are we talking hedge witches or elementals here?"

It was a good question. Most of the hedge witches were really nothing more than witch wannabees. Very few had any actual power. Elementals, like myself and my family, however, were a very different story.

All I could do was shrug. "I don't really know all that much about them, to be honest. Last I looked into them, they were kind of a mix. But a mix lighter on the elemental side of things.

I think they added a lot of locals to boost their numbers to thirteen."

"Power number, huh?" When I nodded, he hesitated for a minute. "Is four a power number? Will I be messing things ups, power-wise, by joining the Gemstone Coven?"

"Nope. Now, if we were three to begin with, that might be a different story. Trinities are powerful. Three, six, nine, and then for some reason it jumps to thirteen for the next power number. Although, now that I think about it, I don't see why twelve wouldn't be just as powerful."

I narrowed my eyes at him. "Are you one hundred percent sure you want to go through with this?" I mean, if he was going to change his mind, the man was running out of time.

He smiled at me. "Absolutely positive. It's the right thing for us going forward. I need to understand how witchcraft really works if we are going to make this work. The only way for me to really do that is to become one myself."

That wasn't entirely true, and I had just opened my mouth to tell him that when the doorbell rang.

"You expecting anyone?" Trevor asked. I shook my head, and we both stood to go answer the door.

The other side of the door presented Oak Hill deputy Steve Brighton.

"Sorry to call so early in the morning, but I didn't want to wait until after work." He held up a rather large brown envelope. "I tried Patty's first, but she wasn't home yet. Would you mind giving her this?" He paused. "And if you all could keep it between yourselves how you came to get this, I'd really appreciate it, too."

"Can I ask what this is?" Trevor asked. Kind of defeating the purpose of the question, if you asked me. Which, of course, he didn't.

Steve hesitated. "I'm guessing that if you all live here on the same property, you are pretty tight friends. Is that right?"

I nodded. Of the five people living here on the estate, Patty was the only one not a part of the family. Well, family in the traditional sense, anyway. Trevor had been in that number until a couple of days ago, but we had all known that status would be changing soon. Now it had.

"Patty is more than a friend," I said. "She's part of our team. I'd trust her with my life." And I had, too. On more than one occasion.

Steve blinked at the team mention but didn't ask the question I'd half expected him to. That was good for me. The team thing had kind of slipped out. I really should get Patty's approval before letting the man into that side of things. She knew him far better than I did.

He reached up to run a quick hand through his hair. "To be honest, I'd be telling you the answer to that, anyway. And that brings me to the next reason I stopped by here."

Then he just stopped talking. I tilted my head at him. "Which was what?"

Steve took a deep breath and then said, "The department isn't letting me in on this one. They know I have a... history... with Patty, and they have warned me to stay off the case."

Trevor looked pointedly at the package in his hands and then back at Steve. "Is that right?"

The man swallowed. "Yes. And no. I didn't follow that to the letter of the law." He nodded to the packet. "That's the coroner's report you're holding. Very interesting reading, I think you'll find. I had to call in more than a single favor to get my hands on that, so I'm hoping it helps Patty put a quick end to this."

Then he raised his eyes to mine, giving me one of those stares that went straight through to your soul. I narrowed my eyes at him. Few normal people could do that. Steve Brighton might just be more than what we knew. But in what way?

"I think she's going to need help to do that. After all, she has her job as sheriff over at Wind's Crossing. That's a time-consuming job, to say the least." He took another deep breath. "I've done my research on you, and I think I want to hire you for this."

Ah, so that was what all this was about. I just shook my head at him.

"I can't take you on as a client on this one."

His entire face shut down. Then he reached for the packet. Trevor moved it the few inches needed to keep the man's hand from grasping it.

"Let her finish," Trevor said.

I smiled at Steve, then dug in my pocket to bring out the quarter I was carrying. Holding it up for him to see, I upped my smile to a grin. "As an ethical detective, I don't take more than one client for a single case. And Patty's already hired me."

Steve looked from me to the quarter and back again, letting that sink in. Finally, his face got a little more expression to it, and he nodded.

"I understand." He glanced over his shoulder back at his car. We were still standing right there at the front door. Where were my manners this morning? "I hate to rush, but I'm on my way to work, so I can't stay long. But I want you to know that if you need my help on this, just ask. There are more jobs out there. There is only one Patty."

And with that, he turned, walked back to his car, and left.

Trevor shut the door after we'd watched the car start down the drive, then turned to me. "That's a man in love right there."

Yeah. That was kind of my take on that scene, too. But then again, it could be just a really good friendship, too. I mean, I'd go to the ends of the earth for a good friend, just as I would for a member of my family. But still... I didn't think that was the case with Steve.

No. I thought just maybe Patty had been holding something back from us. I just didn't know why.

We were still standing right there by the door, pondering our next move, when Trevor's watch went off. And yes, we both jumped.

"What was that for?" I asked.

He shut the alarm off, then looked at me with somewhat panicked eyes. "It's time to get ready for my initiation." He swallowed. "I didn't want to risk being late. You know how your

Aunt Opal is about punctuality, and I don't want to start this off on the wrong foot."

Actually, it was a very good thing he'd set that alarm. As important as this day was to the rest of our future together, with everything going on, I'd have been late for it for sure.

We headed upstairs to shower and change for the event. I rushed to finish first so that I'd be there when Trevor came out of the bathroom to find the package wrapped in plain brown paper waiting for him on the bed.

He lifted it up. "What is this?"

I grinned at him. "Open it and find out."

He did. Then he lifted out the thin black robe from the box's depth. With the hood of the cloak up, it would literally cover him from head to toe.

"For the ceremony?"

I nodded. "And beyond. For the record, we'll all be wearing our robes today. We do that for official occasions. It's an Opal thing. She takes being High Priestess very seriously, you know. Even if our coven is just a family affair."

He nodded, distractedly running a hand down the material of the cloak. "As powerful as your coven is, I think that sounds about right." He hesitated. "So, will we be wearing the cloaks the whole time?"

Yes. There was a definite measure of hope in his voice. I grinned at him. I knew what that hope stemmed from. Witches had a habit of conducting their meetings sky-clad. Which is just a fancy and witchy way of saying stark naked. My Aunt Opal was a big fan of sky-clad meetings. She really didn't want any cloth barriers between her and the Goddess's blessings.

It had caused us problems in the past.

"This is a day meeting, and an initiation to boot, so yes. We'll all be wearing our cloaks the entire time."

His shoulders fell. Trevor had a lot to let go of on his journey to become a true witch. Part of that was letting go of the thought that there was anything wrong with nudity. I mean, the God and Goddess brought us into this world naked, didn't they? It wasn't anything to be ashamed of.

Especially as we kept it in the family. Although, now that I thought about it, that might have been part of the problem with Trevor. We just might have to have a coven discussion about bending the sky-clad rules. At least for the next few months.

I didn't want him backing out because of that one little thing.

There was a host of other reasons he might not make it as a witch, but a simple thing like whether or not we held our meetings dressed or undressed shouldn't be one.

Should it?

Chapter 6

We weren't late. That was what mattered.

Of course, if it hadn't been for Trevor's alarm, we would have been. But that was beside the point. We were on time. If only by the skin of our teeth, we were in place at the bonfire at straight-up noon.

Lack of full moon or not, all of our official coven meetings were held up on the top of the hill behind the old farmhouse. It had been that way for as long as I could remember.

After all, I'd been born in that farmhouse. As had Ruby. On the self-same day, come to think of it. They'd tried hard to make our births simultaneous but had missed it by a matter of seconds.

Ruby had yet to let me live that down. She always stressed that she was the oldest, and thus, the wisest. As if sixty seconds could make a difference in the amount of wisdom gathered.

The others were already in the clearing. There was Opal on the far side of the flames, my cousin Ruby to her right, and my mom across the flames from her. The entire coven in a nutshell. We'd talked about joining together with others from Team Destiny, but in the end, we hadn't.

I rather liked our small, family coven. It was... comfortable. I had to think the others felt the same.

After quickly getting Trevor set up on the spot designated for him, I took a few steps forward to claim my spot on Opal's left. The circle was now complete, and the Gemstone Coven was open for business.

I should note at this point, that I was very glad that Opal had agreed upon the robes beforehand. With the flames of the small bonfire between us, it was rather hot.

Then it wasn't. I caught Opal's small, and thankful, nod to my mom over the fire. Yeah, if my brain wasn't elsewhere, I might have cast the temperature control spell myself. But right now, I wasn't quite thinking straight. I'd feel much better once this was over and done.

When Opal cleared her throat and glanced around the circle, I knew things were about to get started in full. And yes, I was more than a little nervous. I still remembered my first time at the circle, and I'd been raised to this. Still didn't make it any less nerve-racking.

Trevor was still a flight risk.

"Who seeks entry into the circle of the Gemstone Coven?" Opal said. Not in her normal tone of voice, mind you. Not my aunt. There was more than a little power backing up those few, simple words.

I took a deep breath and answered. After all, I was Trevor's guide in this matter. "I bring to you Trevor, my best friend, my soul-mate, and my husband. He wishes to join the coven and to study our craft. For the honor of the Goddess and the betterment of all."

Opal gave a solemn nod, then turned her gaze upon Trevor. So did I. He was still right where I'd left him, and holding up better than what I'd expected. So far, so good.

"Seeker, hast thou decided on thy name for entry into our sacred circle?"

Luckily, Trevor and I had already discussed this part beforehand, so he was expecting it. Ruby and I had used our birth-given names, but then we'd been born into all this. Trevor hadn't.

In a way, this was his second birthday. Well, you get what I mean. He was being born again today. And as he was joining the Gemstone Coven, it only seemed fitting that his name should be that of a gem.

"I seek entry under the name of Onyx, High Priestess." Yeah, there was a reason his robe was black. Ours weren't. We'd all opted for a cloak to match our gemstone. And yes, that made us a colorful group of witches. Just the way we liked it.

Being normal was so overrated.

The corners of Opal's mouth twitched. I thought she rather approved. After all, nothing in the rules said he had to choose a matching gemstone name. But it had been a nice gesture all the same.

"The Goddess has deemed you worthy of entry into our circle." Only the slightest of pauses. "As have we all. Please join the sacred circle of the coven and kneel in the Goddess's presence."

For once, she was speaking figuratively and literally at the same time. No. The Goddess was not standing there with us. However, that didn't mean she wasn't there. She was. Every one of us could feel her presence. And Opal hadn't been kidding about Trevor being deemed worthy by the Goddess, either. She'd made sure to tell us all that personally.

It was up to Trevor to choose his place in the circle. It did not surprise me when he knelt in the space between me and Mom. But he was facing Opal. As our High Priestess, she was the representative of the Goddess for this event.

When Opal spoke again, the power was gone from behind the words. That meant a lot to me. So did the love I could hear in her voice.

"My dearest Onyx, by marrying my niece Amethyst, you have already become part of our greater family. Not that you weren't even before that joyous event ever took place. That being said, with your entry into this coven, you become part of the spiritual side of our family as well. Are you prepared for that and all that entails?"

Trevor, or rather Onyx, nodded solemnly. "I am."

Silence fell for a few seconds as Opal gazed into my mate's eyes. Finally, she continued. "The mysteries of the Goddess are not few in number, Seeker. As such, they are beyond our comprehension in this brief life span we have been given. However, as a dedicated member of this coven, it will be your mission to seek knowledge and grow every day from now until the end of your time on earth. With your willingness, the Goddess will guide you on your journey."

She paused, still holding Trevor's gaze with her own. "Are you prepared to be born anew this day, in the light and blessing of the Goddess herself, and to honor and do her bidding from this day forward?"

I expected a small hesitation on Trevor's part here. This was a big step for him. Huge, even. But he didn't pause at all. He simply nodded.

"I am."

"Then rise, Onyx, newborn child of the Goddess, and be welcomed into the circle as a neophyte of the Gemstone Coven."

One by one, each of us kissed our newest member and presented him with a small gift to help him in his new life. Opal was first, with a chalice to drink in knowledge. Sapphire was next with a mortal and pedestal—essential tools for any witch worth her salt. Then Ruby with a simple wand that she had handcrafted herself. Wands were super useful for those just beginning to learn spellcraft.

That left only me. My kiss didn't fall on the man's cheek as the others' kisses had. Mine was full on the lips. Only afterward did I hand him my gift. His very first athame. All of us had one very similar to this one. The only true difference between them was the gemstone placed with honor in the center of the small blade's hilt. His was a shining black laced with white.

Onyx.

Trevor waited until we were on our way home to ask his question. I was actually glad about that. Better to handle this one in private. Especially after I saw his disappointment with my answer.

"What is a neophyte?"

I considered how to put it into words. Then I just shrugged and said it as simply as I could. "It's kind of a probationary witch."

He tried to hide that disappointment, but yeah, it was there. I'd known him long enough to read it in his face.

"Probationary, huh?"

I reached over and put one hand on his arm. I'd have given the man a hug, but that wasn't really safe as he was driving a moving vehicle at the time.

"It doesn't make what happened today any less than what it appeared to be, you know. We just wanted to give you a way out if this turned out to not be your path, after all."

I hadn't expected the sudden increase of disappointment that flashed in his eyes.

"We? So, making me a probationary member was something you had a part in?"

Oh boy. This could be tricky.

"Yes. It was." I paused, wishing not for the first time for a car with old-fashioned bench seats. Bucket seats wouldn't allow me to get as close to him as I wanted to be right now.

"Look. When Ruby and I joined, we went straight into it without the Neophyte title. But we were born witches. Even if the Moms did make us wait until we were eighteen to officially join the coven, we knew exactly what we were getting into. All of it."

Another, shorter pause. "The truth is, Trevor, you don't. I respect your decision to become a witch and a member of our coven. We all do. But this will be a totally new path for you to follow. Until you have a chance to travel that path, there is truly no way to know that it is the one you should be on. This is your chance to find out."

He swallowed. "Funny, but the ceremony didn't really sound like that at all. It all sounded rather final."

I nodded. "And it can be... if the path proves to be right for you. As you learn the pagan ways and rituals, that will become clear. This just gives you a little space, that's all."

He was keeping his eyes glued to the road. That couldn't be good. We hadn't meant this to hurt his feelings, dang it all.

"So how long before I become a card-carrying member?"

I tried on a small smile. "We don't actually carry cards, you know."

At least that got me a glance, though not a happy one. "You know what I mean."

Yeah, I did. I shrugged. "That's really up to you. And for the record, we'd make anyone joining the coven go through this. It's an important stage. If you tackle this full-on, then you should reach the first level of witchcraft within a matter of a few months. Maybe even sooner."

"First level of witchcraft?"

"That's right. Anyone who passes on to the first full level is no longer considered a neophyte." I hesitated. "Think of it as kind of a preliminary on-the-job training kind of thing."

"And once I reach the first level, the probation is over? I'm a full witch?"

I hesitated. "Yes, and no. The probation is over. That part is a definite yes. And you would be a full member of the coven. But you would not be a full witch. You'd be a level one witch."

He considered that for a minute. "And what level are you and Ruby?"

"We're level two."

The car swerved just a touch. "You've been witches all your lives, and you're only level two?"

I laughed. "I'm only level two because, at least with our coven, there are only three levels. Opal holds the third level. Unless I'm wanting to start my own coven, level two is right where I'll stay. Thank you very much. But I should warn you, there is an enormous difference between levels one and two. Level one you might reach in a few months. Level two? To be honest, as a hedge witch, you might never make it to that level."

My eyes watched his face carefully. "Are you okay with that?"

He nodded slowly. "I suppose if you, with all your power, can be happy with a level two ranking, then I have nothing to complain about with being level one, do I?"

I blew out a breath that I hadn't even realized I'd been holding. One hurdle down.

Only about a million to go.

CHAPTER 7

We'd brought the packet from Steve with us to drop off at Patty's on the way. Then we'd been running so close on time, we hadn't had the chance.

Time to rectify that. I wanted to open it to read in the car. Now that the initiation was over and I could, you know, actually think again. Hadn't Steve said it made for interesting reading? What exactly did that mean?

Was the murder scene not what it appeared to be? Well, I mean, I could have guessed that. Unless Oak Hill had some new weird kind of satanic cult that I didn't know about. And that kind of thing should have crossed onto my radar if that was the case. Not that I could totally rule it out, mind you. But it was unlikely at best.

Especially considering who the victim was. I really didn't believe much in coincidences.

Luckily, she was up when we got there. But not by much. I think we caught her right before she hit the shower.

If she'd thought about asking us to come back later, that thought went bye-bye quick when she heard about the packet. She opened it even as we all made our way into her tiny home. Only then did I think that maybe the better idea would have been to have Patty pick it up at our house. I always forgot just how small her little A-frame was until I stepped into it.

Her seating was limited, so she spread the packet out on her small table for two, and she and I took the seats. Trevor stood between us.

"There's a fold-up stool in the corner," Patty told him.

He went to retrieve it, and Patty started going through the paperwork like a demon. This wasn't her first coroner's report, and it was pretty dang clear that she knew exactly what she was looking for. It didn't take her long to find it, either.

I knew something was up when her mouth dropped open and she said, "Son of a biscuit eater."

Trevor forgot about setting up the stool and went to stand behind Patty. All the better to look over her shoulder that way. I was about to do the same when she finally took pity on me.

"The report is declaring Parson's death as natural causes. According to this, the man died of a heart attack. Not an athame through the heart."

My mouth dropped open, too. How could that be?

Of the three of us, only Trevor didn't seem all that surprised by the news. "I was kind of wondering why there wasn't more blood at the scene. A stabbing should have, well, had a lot more of the red stuff at the site."

I just looked at him. "And you're only mentioning this now because?"

He shrugged. "I didn't get that much time at the crime scene. I couldn't be sure." He hesitated as color filled his cheeks. "Plus, to be honest, my mind hasn't exactly been all that sharp lately."

That I could understand. The man had a lot on his plate right now. I got that.

Patty still didn't look convinced. "I'm not so sure we aren't still looking at murder here," she said slowly. "According to the coroner, Parsons had a history of heart problems. If someone knew that—and everyone close to the man should have—then how hard would it have been to make the man have a coronary event?"

"That makes sense," I agreed. "And thinking you were going to be sacrificed would definitely do the job, I'd think."

While Patty and I had continued the conversation, Trevor had continued his reading. I noticed he was shaking his head.

"I don't think that's what happened," he said.

Patty and I both arched eyebrows at him. We'd be wanting a little more than that, and he had to know that.

Trevor blew out a long breath and pointed to the report still in front of Patty. "The report also mentions that the body appeared to have been moved after death and that according to preliminary testing, the man died at least a couple of hours before the knife was, well, you know."

Patty snatched up the report and read quickly, her eyes narrowing the more she read. Finally, she set the papers back down and looked over at me. "He's right. It's looking like Parsons might have actually died of natural causes, and then someone used his death to try to incriminate me." She paused. "Or, to be a little more open-minded, to incriminate a witch in general."

"I'm not sure that really changes how we investigate this, though, does it?" I asked. "Whoever did this had to be fairly close to Parsons, right?"

Patty nodded slowly. "Right. A couple of hours wouldn't be all that much time to pull this together, when you think about it. So, chances are good they were with the man when he had the heart attack."

"All right then." I looked up at Trevor. "What say you and I go have a little heart to heart with the wife?"

He was already heading for the door. Why speak when action would answer?

Parsons' house was nice. As in, super-duper nice. Not the kind of home you would expect a lowly county commissioner to own. But then again, we didn't know that much about Mrs. Parsons. It was possible the woman had been born into money, right? Although, in a town as small as Wind's Crossing, I was pretty sure I'd have heard that little tidbit before now. The rumor mill was strong here.

When Mrs. Parsons opened the front door, I noticed two things immediately. The first was that the woman was knock-down, drag-out gorgeous. Not what I'd been expecting with Parsons' reputation for having affairs. Why go afield when you had a wife that looked like a supermodel?

The second thing was that Mrs. Parsons did not appear to be a grieving widow. At all.

She actually smiled at us, and her eyes were dry. The wine glass she was holding, however, wasn't.

"Let me guess. You're looking into my husband's death, too, aren't you?"

As I said, the rumor mill was strong in Wind's Crossing. Most people kept up with the goings-on in the Ravenswind family. That meant they knew of my new career as a private investigator.

"We are," I said. Then I nodded past her into the house. "Do you mind if we come in and have a little talk with you?"

She stepped aside and motioned with her hand, almost spilling her wine as she did so. It was enough to make me think that just maybe that wasn't her first glass of the evening.

Trevor and I followed her into a spacious front room with a large wall of windows on one side and a massive fireplace on the other. In between the two was a rather eclectic selection of seating options. Mrs. Parsons sat in one of the comfier-looking chairs, and we sat on the sofa across from it.

With none of the furniture actually matching, you'd think it would lend a shabby air to the room, but you'd be wrong. This had to have been done by a designer. It worked a little too well to have been an accident.

"So, what can I help you with?" she asked. Then she leaned in. "Haven't they arrested that witch of a sheriff yet? I mean, it's fairly obvious she was involved, isn't it?"

So much for keeping an open mind about the general witch thing, huh?

"No. Sheriff Bluespring has not been arrested. It isn't exactly normal to arrest people who are obviously being framed," Trevor said.

The woman leaned back and took a sip of wine. "Framed?"

"That would appear to be the case, yes," I said. I was pretty sure we didn't want to go into the whole heart attack thing with the woman. For one, we didn't want to put our cards on the table like that. And for two, we weren't exactly supposed to know about that, were we?

She stared at us for a few seconds and then nodded slowly. "Of course, you are witches, too, aren't you? You'd have to think that, wouldn't you?"

Trevor straightened a little more on the sofa. "I've been a lawman for all my adult life, Mrs. Parsons. And when I look into a case, I think you should know that I look at the facts. I leave personal feelings out of it."

She gave a small smile and a little giggle. "Of course you do, dear. I'm sorry to have implied otherwise." She took another sip from the glass she was holding. "But you know that my husband was about to have her fired from her position as sheriff, don't you?"

Trevor met her eyes dead-on. "I know he was going to try."

You could have cut the tension in the room at that point with a knife. An athame, to be exact. Time to step in and get back on track. I mean, we already knew Patty was innocent, so this talk wasn't getting us anywhere we wanted to go.

"We actually didn't come here to talk about Patty," I said as calmly as I could manage. "Do you know of anyone else who would have wished your husband harm?"

She laughed, and there wasn't an ounce of mirth to it. "Besides me, you mean?"

I glanced at Trevor and then back at her, but didn't say anything. This wasn't the time for words. Silence worked better.

"No. I will not pretend that we had the perfect marriage. We didn't. Johnny had a wandering eye toward the women, and it isn't easy being the talk of the town in that way. I can assure you of that. Plus, he lets our daughters get by with murder, and now they have a criminal record. A criminal record! I try to instill discipline, but why even try when all they have to do is run to their father and have him say yes to whatever they want?"

It was hard to keep my emotions from showing, but I tried. "That couldn't have been easy to handle as a wife and a mother. It must have caused a very strained relationship between the two of you."

She gave another mirthless laugh. "You can say that again. There were times I hated the jerk." She must have realized she went too far with that one, circumstances being what they were. "But he was my husband and the father of my children. Besides, I had my own way of dealing with his infidelities." Mrs. Parsons leaned in a little toward us and lowered her voice. "Two can play that game, you know."

It didn't much sound like a game I'd want to play, personally, but I kept that thought to myself. Instead, I just went on with the questions. "Please don't take this the wrong way, Mrs. Parsons, but we have to ask. Where were you the night your husband... died?" I just couldn't bring myself to say the murdered word when I knew better. Luckily, she didn't seem to catch it.

She leaned back again in her chair, a gloating look on her face. "Right here at home with my daughters. Where Johnny should have been, too. If he had been, well, then he'd still be alive right now, wouldn't he?"

"All right, then," Trevor said, with a glance at me. "You were home with the girls. Which brings us back to that question of who, other than you, might want to harm Mr. Parsons." He paused. "Do you know any of the women he was having affairs with?"

She grimaced and looked away. "I tried very hard to not know that, thank you very much." Then she paused, draining her glass in the interim. After setting it down on the small table beside her, she finally looked back. Her eyes were cold as ice. All pretense of being friendly was gone. "But you do know the man wasn't a very honest accountant, don't you? You might want to talk with that boss of his."

Mrs. Parsons paused with a thoughtful look. "And maybe have a little chat with that wife of his, too, while you're at it." She gave a little dry laugh and then stood. "And now, I have to get ready for my Tai Chi lesson. The master will be here in a few minutes, and I'm not even dressed for it yet."

The way she said the word master sent chills down my spine. I had to wonder if maybe the 'master' was one of the ways she got even with her husband. Well, late husband now.

Might be worth having a little talk with him, too. But not today.

CHAPTER 8

There was a small package on our front porch when we got home. We'd stopped off for dinner on the way. After all, this was kind of our honeymoon period, and our vacation, to boot. Eating out was part of that.

Not to mention the fact that we'd both had a rather full day, and neither of us felt quite up to cooking. That played into it too.

Trevor hefted the box. There was no address label on it at all. There wouldn't be if it was what I thought it was. He arched his eyebrows at me.

"You think it's safe to open?"

I grinned at him and leaned in to take a whiff of the brown paper wrapping. Only then did I nod. I mean, it pays to be careful, right? We did have some pretty powerful enemies out there. But that paper had the distinct aroma of Mom's favorite perfume all over it.

"I'd say so," I said. "But let's go inside first."

To be honest, I was more than a little curious about the contents of that package. I mean, I knew it had to be a starter kit of sorts for a beginning witch. But I wasn't sure what that meant for a hedge witch. It was out of my realm of knowledge. Mom must have been doing a little research on just that. It said something that Opal had handed that task over to Mom.

It was kind of a big deal, mentoring a new witch. It was nice to know that Mom had my back.

Trevor set the box on the kitchen table and looked at it for a few seconds before taking a deep breath and tearing off the paper. By that time, I was pretty sure he had a good guess as to what this was. He opened the box and took out two books.

The first was a slim volume filled with pictures and space to take notes in the margins. A beginner's guidebook to witch-craft.

Trevor thumbed through the book, his smile growing with each page he turned. Finally, he looked over at me with a rather cocky grin. "This is going to be a lot easier than I thought it would be. This is mostly just plants and herbs and stuff. I learned all that stuff a long time ago. I was an Eagle Scout, you know."

I nodded. I hated to burst his bubble so soon, but it had to be done. "That's just the very first guidebook, you know." I shrugged and smiled to try to soften the coming blow. "It's kind of the remedial starting point."

"Oh." His face fell, then brightened. "You know what? I'm still counting this as a win."

That was my fella, all right. Always looking on the brighter side of things. And why not? It was a win. A definite jump on the witch's learning curve, at the very least. That wasn't anything to sneeze at now that I thought about it.

Then he picked up the other book. "What's this one?"

"That's your first grimoire."

Was it my imagination, or did his face just get a little whiter? Yeah, a lot of people had the wrong idea about grimoires.

With more than a little trepidation, he opened it and flipped through a few pages. Then his eyes met mine. "It's empty."

"Well, duh. This is your first day as a witch. Of course, it's empty." Then I took pity on him. I had to remember he was new to this side of things. "A grimoire is a very personal thing. It's a witch's spellbook, but it's also a kind of journal. Where we keep notes of things we learn that might come in handy at a later date. It's also where we keep our recipes."

He gave me an unbelieving look. "Recipes? Really?"

I swatted at his arm. "Not like meatloaf or chili. Recipes for medicines and things. Not all magic is magic, you know. Although if you have healing power like Mom, using a medicinal recipe can pack a bigger punch." I paused. "Actually, when you think about it, spells and potions are really nothing more than recipes at the very basic level of things."

He closed the book and ran his hand over its cover. "This is a nice one."

Well, yeah, it would be if Mom picked it out. Going with a black leather cover had been a thoughtful touch. As had been the Onyx gemstone at the center of the pentagram. Mom had been quick on the uptake for that one.

The next morning was an early one. You would think with the coroner's report coming back with a verdict of natural causes, our job would basically be done. I mean, even if witches did sacrifice people (and we don't), there wasn't much good in sacrificing a dead man, now was there?

So that should have brought Patty off the hot plate, right? According to Trevor, wrong. When he had checked his email before bed, he'd found out that Mrs. Parsons was taking up where her husband had left off. The county meeting to decide Patty's fate was still on.

That meant we were too.

Parsons' employer was the Midwest Limestone Fabricators company just outside of Oak Hill. The early rising part was because they opened early, and we wanted a chance to have our little talk before the owner got too caught up in his daily activities.

I'll admit, I hadn't known what to expect. I mean, sure, I'd seen some pretty buildings built out of limestone. But dang. I had no idea that building with the grayish-white stone was such a popular thing. The size of the establishment we pulled into, however, said it was.

We followed the signs to end up at the smaller office building. In a matter of minutes, we were seated in front of Thomas Klein's large, and rather impressive, desk. The man was smiling at us as he leaned over that desk to talk to us.

"So, I take it the two of you are interested in building your new home with limestone?"

Ah. That would explain the speedy process of getting in to see him. Not to mention the big, friendly smile.

"Actually, no," I said. "We're here to talk to you about an employee of yours. Johnny Parsons."

His big smile faltered, then disappeared altogether. "I see. And how do you think I can help you with that?"

Klein's eyes skipped over me and went on to Trevor. Normally that would bother me, as I was the one who had spoken. But not today. I got it. Even without his uniform on, Trevor reeked of his law enforcement persona. People tended to see the uniform even when it wasn't there. And if that helped us in this case, well, then why look a gift horse in the mouth?

"Can you tell us if Johnny was close with any of the men working here for you? Or women either, for that matter," Trevor asked.

Klein was a pretty good actor, but I could tell the question bothered him. A bobbing Adam's apple would tell on a man just about every time.

He leaned back in his chair and looked at us for a minute. "I take it neither of you really knew Johnny all that well, did you?"

"Why do you say that?" I asked.

Klein shook his head. "Johnny may have worked here, but he always thought he was above us. To include me." He reached out a finger and made a dust trail on his desk. "Fabricating limestone is a very dusty affair. The workers out in the mill look more like statues than men by the end of the day. Johnny thought he deserved a cleaner working environment."

"Then why did he work here? The man was a Certified Public Accountant, wasn't he? I would think he could get a job in a... cleaner environment if he wanted to."

Klein chuckled. "Not at what I was paying him, he couldn't. I compensated for the environment rather well." The chuckle died, and he paused to give us another brief stare before going on. "I'm probably putting myself into the position of lead suspect, but Johnny wasn't a very good employee. When he... died... I had to bring in another accountant."

He cleared his throat and there was more Adam's apple dancing. "It would appear that good old Johnny had been skimming money from me for years. A substantial amount of money, too." His eyes met Trevor's. "But I swear I didn't know that until after. If I'd known before, the man would be in jail rather than in a mortuary right now."

It wasn't all that great of news for our investigation, but I believed him. So much for a quick case resolution, huh?

That didn't, however, mean that we were done talking with Mr. Klein. Far from it. I remembered how wonky Mrs. Parson's eyes had gone when she had told us to talk to the wife too. I was thinking maybe the woman hadn't been so truthful about not knowing who Parsons' current affairs were with.

Even as I was opening my mouth to go in that direction, Trevor beat me to it. Sometimes I forgot he does this sort of thing for a living, too.

"Does your wife work in the business too? We'll need to talk to her as well."

Klein straightened a little in his chair. "Glenda wouldn't be able to tell you any more than I already have. There isn't any need to drag her into all this."

Trevor looked at the man for a long, hard minute. That lawman's stare would get them almost every single time. This time was no exception to the rule.

Klein's shoulders finally slumped, and he let out a long breath. "All right, all right. A murder investigation, right? Pulling out all the stops, and all that... I get it." Another long breath. "To answer your question, yes, she works in the business. But she is rarely in the office. She prefers to work from home."

He gave a rueful smile. "Less dust there, you know. Although if we didn't have a housekeeper, that might not be the case."

I didn't miss Trevor's side glance over at me. Hey. There were worse things in life than a little dust. But maybe I should start upping my housekeeping game. Either that or check into getting a housekeeper a few days a week myself.

"Can we get your home address, please?" Trevor asked.

Klein squirmed. Actually squirmed right there in his chair. I was getting a nagging feeling that he didn't much care for the thought of us talking to his wife about Johnny Parsons. Which, of course, only meant there had to be an excellent reason for us to do exactly that.

"Um. I'll give you the address. I don't have a problem with that. Only..." His voice trailed off. It was a little stronger when it started back up again. "You won't find her there, I'm afraid.

She's off visiting her mother." He paused. "I think they went to a resort somewhere, but to be honest, I'm not sure she told me the name. Sorry."

Yeah. The man didn't look sorry at all.

I would have stood up at that point, thinking we were done here, but I noticed Trevor was still sitting pretty solid in his chair. Maybe we weren't done after all.

"I still want that address," he said. Then, as Klein scribbled that down on a scrap piece of paper, he continued. "And I'll be wanting your wife's cell phone number, too."

Color flushed into Klein's cheeks, but he added the number onto the sheet. "No problem giving you her number, but it isn't going to do any good, I'm afraid. Glenda is very forgetful about carrying her phone. She left it on the kitchen table."

"In that case, I'd appreciate your mother-in-law's number, if you have it."

Klein grimaced. "Sorry. I don't. The woman never much cared for me, so I really had no reason to ever call her, did I? I left that communication to Glenda."

Trevor nodded, took the paper, and then stood. I followed.

"If you think of anything that might help with the investigation into Parson's death, I'd appreciate a call." He handed the man one of my business cards.

Okay, so now we were done.

CHAPTER 9

We hadn't even made it off the man's parking lot before my cell phone chirped. Unlike Mrs. Klein, at least I had my phone with me. It was a good thing I did, too.

"I thought of something else." Klein didn't beat around the bush or start off with the generally accepted way of beginning with hello or even an introduction as to who was calling. Luckily, I recognized his voice. "Parsons did a bit of pro-bono work for the local animal shelter. I remember thinking how out of character it was for the man to give his time so freely, without payment. Now that I know the true situation here, I have to wonder if the man was skimming from them, too."

"You think Parsons was stealing from the animal shelter?" Don't get me wrong, I don't like crooks stealing, period. But crooks stealing from poor, unfortunate animals that needed every cent they could get? That was wrong on an upgraded number of levels, that was.

"Don't have proof of that, no. But it's the only explanation I can come up with as to why Parsons would be willing to work for free. And if I'm right... well, there are a fair few activist types that work at that shelter. And sometimes activists can get pretty riled up. Just saying, you might want to check it out. Maybe they found out about that skimming thing before I did."

"Thank you. We'll check into it." I ended the call and looked over at Trevor. As I'd taken the call on speakerphone, he'd heard both sides of the conversation.

"What do you think?" I asked him.

He shrugged and shook his head. "Truthfully, it's hard to say. This might just be Klein's way of getting us off his wife's trail."

Yeah, that was kind of my thinking, too. But on the other hand, Klein was right about Parsons not being the kind of man to do community work with nothing to gain from it.

"Still worth checking out, though, right?"

He nodded. "Oh, heck yeah."

We stopped for a quick bite to eat at the Flour Pot. The early morning hour was against us now, as the shelter didn't open to the public for another half hour. What better way to fill that time than with donuts and coffee?

But at nine o'clock sharp, when they unlocked the shelter's front door, Trevor and I were standing right there waiting.

The man just blinked at us for a minute, then smiled. "Sorry, we don't usually have a line waiting for us to open. I'm hoping that's a good thing. We have a lot of animals needing homes right now. Are you looking for a cat, a dog, or one of our other animal varieties?"

I had to know. "You have other animal varieties?"

He nodded. "We sure do. Right now, we happen to have a ferret, a couple of parakeets, and a bearded dragon. Dogs and cats are the most frequent animal given up to us, but we generally get a few others too."

"Good to know." It was too bad we all had our familiars sorted out. Maybe I'd have to put a bug in the ear of the witches' council that the animal shelter would be a good place for anyone looking.

The life of a familiar might be a hard one, but it had its rewards, too. And it sure as heck would beat living out one's life in a shelter. Most of the familiars I knew were pretty darn pampered creatures. They earned it.

The man held his hand out to me. "I'm Jeff Lee, manager of this place."

My eyebrows went up. "Morgan's dad? I'm Amie Ravenswind, Ruby's cousin."

He gave me a smile that actually seemed genuine. It was a pleasant change of pace. Most of the time, people weren't all that happy when we turned their errant, bond-jumping children back over to the law.

"I thanked Ruby already, and now I get to thank you in person. I truly appreciate you two getting Morgan back into the system. She needs to go through the process and learn the consequences of her actions." He shook his head. "Though I am sorry for all the trouble she caused the two of you. Caused everyone, really."

Yeah. And he didn't know the half of it. At least I hoped he didn't. As he wasn't laughing, I had to think that Ruby was keeping the rest of that story in the family. Well, and the area witches too. It was too good of a story not to share with them.

It would be a long while before I could be seen at the council without snickering following me around the whole time.

"I'm just glad she has someone like you that wants what's best for her." I meant that too. "But back to your previous question, we aren't here to adopt, I'm afraid. We're here because we were told that Johnny Parsons volunteered time here as your accountant?" I made it a question right there at the end.

He nodded, glancing behind him as he did. Then he ushered us in and over to a small side room. His office was nothing like the grand affair that Klein's had been. But then, I had to say it was a whole lot cleaner. I'd take clean and small over large and dusty any day of the week.

Once we were all seated, he looked over the small desk at me. "Parsons came in twice a week to catch up on our books. I'm afraid we didn't need him more than that." He lifted his hands in front of him. "Not much coming in, I'm afraid. We're barely able to keep afloat."

"What about that fundraiser you all had last month? That was a pretty popular event, according to the paper," Trevor said.

Lee shook his head. "Unfortunately, once all the bills were paid, there was very little profit left over. Sad really, after all the effort we all put into it."

Trevor's eyes met mine. It had to be said.

"It might be worth having another accountant take a look at the books for that event," I said slowly. "Rumor has it that Parsons wasn't the most honest of men."

Lee's eyes flew up to meet mine. "You think he was stealing from the shelter?"

I had to consider my words. Even witches didn't like talking evil about the dead. "I think it's worth checking into. I was at that event. A lot of people were, and they were spending pretty freely too, for the cause. You should have seen a good profit from that."

He ran a hand through his hair. "Maybe you're right. I know that's been bugging me. I'll call someone else in to take a look. Though, if he did steal from the event, I don't know what could be done about it now."

"Lots of things, actually," Trevor said. "If the man stole from the shelter, then you can make a claim on his estate. You might be able to get reimbursed."

I thought of the super nice house the Parsons lived in, and all the privileges they were freely given because of the man's position on the board of commissioners. It didn't sit well with me. I didn't like the thought of one thing being bought by them with money that should have been spent on the animals here.

Lee brightened. "Wouldn't that be nice?" Then he took a breath. "So, what can I help you with today? I'm afraid I didn't know Parsons all that well. He generally came in after the shelter had closed up for the day."

Gee. I wondered why that was.

"Was there anyone that worked here that knew him better?" I asked.

He hesitated but finally nodded. "In fact, there is. You will probably want to have a talk with Betty. But please be gentle with her. She's taking the man's death pretty hard."

"Why?" I mean, I could guess, but a little confirmation was never a bad thing.

He shook his head. "That's for her to tell you, not me."

Fair enough.

When we finally tracked Betty down, it was to find her in a small fenced-in lot at the back of the facility. She was working with a large German Shepherd. It appeared that she was trying to get her to play.

She didn't seem all that interested in playing to me. In fact, in all my life, I didn't think I'd ever seen a dog look so very sad. It just about broke my heart.

I'd tried hard to not look at the animals we had passed to get to Betty. They all had sad stories, and it made me want to cry just to think of them. I'd take them all home with me if I could. But I wasn't the only one living at our place. I had others to think of, too.

But dang, this was hard. And with this big gal, it was even harder. I wondered what her story was. Then again, I probably didn't want to know. This was hard enough as it was.

Betty heard us coming and looked up. Then the Shepherd looked over at us too. Unless I imagined it, and I don't think I did, her ears perked up just the tiniest bit when her eyes fell on Trevor.

It was hard, but I pushed that thought out of my mind. We were here to talk with Betty, not fawn over the dog. Even if the latter sounded like a much more pleasant way to spend our time.

I realized Trevor had stopped his forward progress and was looking at me. "You think you can handle this interview on your own?"

Tilting my head, I just looked at him. "Sure," I said. "But may I ask why?"

He casually lifted one shoulder. "Well, for one, it might be easier for Betty to open up about an affair without me around. You know, a woman-to-woman kind of thing."

"And for two?"

He took a deep breath and nodded toward the dog, who was now staring directly at him. "She looks like she could use a good long walk. And I'm not sure Betty could handle her if she decided to break away. She might not be getting much in the way of exercise here."

Two excellent points. "Don't go too far, okay?"

He nodded, then after a moment's conversation with Betty, she produced a leash and a grateful smile. The dog and Trevor left to take a long walk out to the main road and back, and I settled in for a little chat with the girl left behind.

It was hard to think of her as a woman, although she had to be fairly close to my own age. She was such a tiny little thing. My heart hardened against Parsons just that little bit more.

We watched the other two disappear from sight, then Betty turned to me. "This is about Johnny, isn't it?"

I nodded. "I've been told that you and Johnny were close. May I ask how close?"

She sniffed, then sighed. "We were in love." Her eyes flitted to my face and then away. "I know it's wrong to love a married man, but he was just waiting until after the next election. Then he was going to get a divorce and move on with me. We were looking at houses and everything."

A part of me wondered if that had been a ploy the man used to gain her trust. I couldn't really see him giving up the nice home he already had. Or any of the money he'd lose in a messy divorce, either. From what I'd read about him, the man wasn't the type to let go of things he possessed.

"When was the last time you saw Johnny?"

She sat down on the ground, her hand running over the short grass at her side. After a few seconds, and a quick ground check for doggy droppings, I sat next to her.

Finally, she answered. "About a week ago. Getting together was hard for us, because Johnny was so very busy with all his volunteer work—and, of course, his work for the county. So we had a set night every week to see each other and look at houses."

Her fingers plucked a blade of grass, and she rubbed it against her cheek with her eyes closed. "We'd take a long drive and look at the area houses that had come onto the market, and then we'd head back to his office."

I had to know. "How did he explain his weekly absence to his wife?"

She blushed and shrugged. "He worked over a lot. With his day job and this place taking up so much of his daytime hours, it wasn't all that unusual for him to spend the night at his office.

Nights were really about the only time he had to do Commissioner stuff."

Yeah. Like that's what he used the office for. Sounded more like it was his little love nest to me. I had to wonder how the county would feel about Parsons if that little fact had gotten out while he was still alive.

"Which night was your standing date?"

"Tuesday. Every Tuesday." A single tear slipped down her cheek. "It was my happiest day of the week. Now it's my saddest."

Ah, crapsnackles. Today was Tuesday.

"I'm sorry, but I have to ask. Did Johnny seem okay to you when you saw him last? Was anything bothering him? Did he seem to be in good health?"

If that last question was a little odd, all things being considered, she didn't catch it. She just nodded.

"Johnny was strong as a horse. Never sick a single day that I knew of. And yeah, I mean, there was always something bothering him. Being stuck in a loveless marriage and having everyone from the county trying to pull you over to their side of issues would do that, wouldn't it?"

"Anything in particular bothering him recently?"

She gave another small shrug. "I wouldn't know. Johnny said our time was so short together, he really didn't want to spend it talking, you know?"

I wanted to gag at the thought, but yeah, I knew all right.

We talked for a few more minutes, mostly waiting for Trevor and Jesse to get back to us. It was pretty clear to me that even though the girl professed love for Parsons, she'd never really known the man at all. She'd been in love with the idea of being in love, I thought.

Trevor and Jesse finally came into sight, and I gathered up the courage to ask the single remaining question that I wanted answered for my own curiosity. "Just for the record, what was it about Johnny Parsons that made him so attractive to women?"

She gave me a disbelieving look. "Didn't you ever meet him? I mean, if you'd met him, you'd know, right?" Betty closed her eyes and took a deep breath. "He was just like a younger Tom Selleck. Not the older version, but back in the Magnum days."

She hugged herself. "Everything about him was absolutely perfect."

Okay, now I had to get out of there before I said something I'd truly regret later. That man had been about as far from perfect as anyone I'd ever heard of.

I stood up, brushing errant grass and dirt from the seat of my jeans as Trevor opened the gate and brought Jesse in. It might have just been my imagination, but Jesse seemed to have a little more spring in her step now than she'd had when they left.

The walk had done her good. Hopefully, the shelter could find a good volunteer to see that Jesse got daily walks. She would need that. I'd be sad, too, if I was stuck in a cage or fence all day long.

Trevor disconnected the leash from Jesse's collar and handed it to Betty, then looked at me. "You all finished with your talk?"

I nodded. Seeing Trevor's hand on Jesse's head and her adoring eyes staring up at him was almost more than I could handle.

I needed to get out of there.

And fast.

Chapter 10

As luck would have it, I was the one driving today. Normally, Trevor takes that duty, but today he seemed a little preoccupied with his phone.

I got that. Patty's situation worried me too, and to be honest, what with him being her deputy and all, Trevor was a lot closer to her than I was. And no, that didn't bother me. I trusted my mate. I also didn't think Patty was the mate-stealing kind of woman, either. If I did, things would be different.

As I pulled out of the shelter's driveway, I glanced over at Trevor. Yup. Already on his phone surfing the net.

"Anything interesting?" I asked.

He sighed and put the phone down. "No. I've been checking into our arrest and call logs from the station. If Parsons' death really was from a heart attack, then why did they find him out in the middle of the woods with a witch's dagger in his chest? It just doesn't make any sense. Especially with the coroner's report showing that his body had been moved. He didn't die on that stone slab."

I was quiet for a minute. He was right, but we both knew that. The only way any of this made sense was if someone was trying to implicate Patty. Or technically, they could be trying to implicate witches in general. But with Patty's history with Parsons, I was fairly certain she was the target here.

"So the man had a heart attack and died," I said, thinking out loud. "Then someone nearby him at the time decided to take advantage of his death and ruin Patty. But who would do such a thing?"

He shrugged. "I don't know. No one that I'd care to be friends with, that's for sure. It's just plain sick."

Well, yeah. That was a given.

His brows furrowed. "Could it be pack-related? I know that Patty has said her mixed blood has caused her problems with the pack before. Could this be their way of getting her out of the picture?"

I thought carefully before answering. "But she isn't an Alpha of the pack. She doesn't have any leadership in a pack that I know of. In fact, I think she's more of an honorary member than anything. Going to this length to hurt her doesn't sound like it would have any upside for all the risk they had to take doing it."

Trevor blew out a breath. "You're right. I'm just grasping at straws here."

He turned to look out the side window for a minute, then actually turned in the seat to face me. Uh-oh. That probably meant that he wanted to see my reaction to whatever he had to say next. And, for some reason, I just didn't think that could be a good thing.

"Do hedge witches need familiars too?"

The car swerved just the tiniest bit. Okay, so I hadn't been expecting that. If nothing else was true of my mate, he was definitely one to keep me on my toes.

I glanced over at him. His eyes and expression were dead serious. This wasn't just a frivolous question. This meant something. And I thought I could take a wild guess at what.

Finally, I nodded. "If they want to be decently strong they do, yes. In fact, it's doubly important for them, as they have a limited amount of power to work with."

Then I waited. I wanted him to be the one that said it, not me. Even if every fiber of my being was aching to just blurt it out. But familiars were a very personal thing. It had to come from him. I could be reading the situation wrong.

But I wasn't.

"Would there be anything wrong with a German Shepherd?" He paused. "Like maybe Jesse?"

I couldn't stop my grin, even as I pulled off the road to make it easier to do the U-turn. "Nothing at all."

Mr. Lee seemed a bit surprised by our knock at his office door. After all, we'd been gone less than ten minutes.

"Did you forget something?" he asked.

"Not exactly," Trevor said. "We'd like to adopt a dog."

Lee grinned at us. "That's wonderful!" He pulled out a packet of papers from his desk drawer. "Do you already have one in mind? Or would you like a tour to pick one out?"

"We want Jesse," I said. I mean, there wasn't any need to draw this out, was there? We knew exactly what dog we wanted.

Lee's smile faltered. "Jesse?"

Trevor just looked at him. "Is there a problem?"

The man took a deep breath, tapping his pen on the top of his desk. "To be honest, we weren't sure we'd be offering Jesse up for adoption. That shepherd has a lot of problems. Physical and emotional."

"I noticed the limp when she walked," Trevor said. "What's her story? Was she abused?"

Not that it mattered to us. Yes, a history of abuse would mean we'd have to give the dog more time to settle in with us. But it sure as heck wasn't a deal-breaker.

Lee leaned back in his chair, scrubbing at his chin. "That's just it. We don't have any way to know that for sure. She's a complete mystery. The vet that handed her over to us said she'd been brought in to him to be put down after a hit-and-run accident. He saw a spark of life in her and decided to save her instead. According to him, it wasn't a simple task."

He made sure he had eye contact with Trevor. "She's going to need a lot of work. Ongoing physical therapy, for one thing. And a lot of time to figure out things emotionally again, too."

"You think it was really a hit and run? Or was she beaten?"

Lee shrugged. "The vet said most of the injuries were consistent with a vehicle hit."

"Most?" I asked.

He nodded. "Yup. That's what he said. Right before he clammed up and stopped talking." Lee shook his head. "He drove quite a distance to bring her to me. We were the closest no-kill shelter that had an opening. Times are tough for homeless animals right now."

"She looked full-bred to me," I said slowly, thinking my way through my words for once. "Didn't she have a chip to trace her back to her owners?"

He gave a short bark of a laugh. "Oh, there's a chip all right. Only it leads to a blank record." He met my gaze. "That isn't supposed to be possible, by the way."

Okay, so poor little Jesse definitely had a past. I glanced over at Trevor. I could tell by his expression that he felt the same way I did. All this only made me want the dog more. Jesse deserved a second chance, dang it all.

"If we agreed to give her physical therapy, and all the emotional support she could possibly need, would you agree to let us adopt her?" Trevor asked.

I was kind of surprised to find myself holding my breath. This morning, I had no thoughts of owning a dog, and now it seemed a very important thing. Plus, my mom could do more for the poor creature than any physical therapist ever could. Mom was the best magical healer I'd ever known.

Maybe a touch of magic was just what Jesse needed the most.

Lee's silence wasn't all that reassuring. Finally, he sighed. "Do you have a fenced-in yard for her to run? Are there other animals in your home?"

Crapsnackles. I hadn't thought about that. How would Destiny feel about a huge and furry big siser? Most likely, she'd be fine with it, but now that the thought came up, it would have behooved me to ask her opinion first.

Then again, the Goddess worked in mysterious ways. What were the chances that the very person we'd needed to talk to here would be working with Jesse when we arrived? That had the scent of the Goddess all over it, if you asked me. And as Destiny was part Goddess... well, that should help me, right?

Trevor was frowning. "Are you saying that Jesse isn't good with other animals? That she's aggressive?"

Lee hesitated. "She has shown no signs of aggression here, no. But you have to consider your other pets. Jesse isn't a small dog, in case you didn't notice. A lot of pets would be intimidated by her."

Trevor was staring at me. "What do you think?"

I chewed on my lip for a few seconds before answering. When I did, my answer was a question for Lee. "Do you allow people to take dogs home to meet the rest of the family before adoption?"

Lee still didn't seem to be on board with the whole adoption thing, but he finally gave a nod. "But the shelter would be up for a lot of liability if things went wrong with this. As I said, Jesse isn't a small dog. Even injured as she is, she could still do a lot of damage if her mind was set on it. And the shelter couldn't survive a lawsuit."

"Don't you have a waiver for that?" Trevor asked.

Lee gave a small smile. "As a matter of fact, I do." He pulled an additional sheet of paper out onto his desk. Then he looked up at Trevor. "But I don't believe you answered me about the fenced-in yard. Jesse would need that, for sure."

"We don't have one... yet," I said. "But if Jesse and our other critters get along, we can rectify that very quickly. And my cousin does have a fenced yard, and it's just a few short steps from our back door."

"And I'll walk her at least twice a day until we get the fence up and going. Long walks." There was just a hint of pleading in Trevor's voice.

Lee's hesitation lasted for another full minute, then he slid the waiver over to us. "Sign the waiver and take Jesse home for a meet and greet. Then we'll talk about going further."

Sounded like a plan to me.

As luck would have it, it was Betty herself who brought Jesse to us in Lee's office. By that time we had finished signing all the paperwork... and there was a lot of paperwork. Who knew that adopting a dog had so much red tape? Especially since the formal adoption paperwork wasn't part of the morning's process. But according to Lee, the papers we did this morning would vastly speed the process when it came to that time.

I think he knew as well as we did that we'd be back to make it official very, very soon.

Betty didn't hand the leash over to Trevor immediately. Instead, she hesitated, with a backward glance at Mr. Lee. "Is it okay if I walk him out to their car?"

Lee nodded, and the three of us left his office.

She waited until we were out of the building before speaking. "I thought of a couple more things, too. I was about to call you when I heard you were back to take Jesse."

"What you were going to call us about?" I asked.

Betty took a deep breath. "I think Johnny was going to call off his other affair the night he was killed." She paused. "I can't prove that, but when he called to tell me goodnight, he wasn't at home."

"So you knew he was having another affair besides you?" Trevor's voice held a touch of disbelief. How little self-confidence did this poor girl have?

"It wasn't a serious affair like ours. And Johnny promised me he was going to break it off."

Yeah, and he was going to divorce his wife, too, I'd bet. I couldn't believe the man had really intended to do either of those things, honestly. It was far more likely that he was just telling the girl what she wanted to hear. Scum like Johnny Parsons was like that.

"Do you have any idea who the other affair was with?"

She shook her head. "Johnny wouldn't tell me." Her blush deepened. "But if I had to guess, I'd say you might want to talk with Mrs. Klein from the limestone mill."

"What makes you think it was her?" Trevor asked.

Betty shrugged. "Johnny could have had his choice of jobs. I mean, CPAs are kind of scarce in these parts. Why would he work at a dusty place like that mill unless there was something—or someone—there that drew him to it?"

Well, according to Klein, the reason he was working there was a more than adequate paycheck. But I didn't want to burst the girl's bubble. Not when she was being so very helpful to us.

Besides, deep down, I kind of thought she might be right. I really wanted a long conversation with Mrs. Klein.

"And the other thing?" Trevor asked gently.

The girl shrugged. "I hate to mention this one, really, but I think maybe you need to look into the sheriff of Wind's Crossing. Lisa Parsons—Johnny's wife—was livid about her arresting their girls. She was pushing Johnny to have her removed from her position. That couldn't have sat well with the sheriff, could it?"

Her eyes raised to mine with a lot of moisture in them. "And what with how he was found...." Her voice trailed off. "I'm sorry," she said. And then she left us. Most likely to have a good cry about it all.

It was too bad that Johnny Parsons was already dead. I really would have enjoyed employing a good old-fashioned Karma spell on the man.

Chapter 11

It took us a good while to get home from the shelter. Neither of us foresaw any problems with keeping Jesse, and we wanted to be prepared. We wanted to help her feel at home right from the very start.

So a trip to the local pet store and a loaded down car later—thank the Goddess we were in Trevor's SUV—we finally made it home. Only to find Patty sitting on our doorstep.

Literally.

"We have swings and rocking chairs, you know," I told her as we walked toward her. Sue me, but I was a big lover of the whole country porch thing. It was a big part of what had made me fall in love with this place to begin with.

She gave a small nod. "Didn't feel much like swinging. Or rocking, either, for that matter." Her words were for me, but her eyes weren't on mine. Or me at all. They were on Jesse.

I glanced over at the dog, now sitting calmly at Trevor's feet. Jesse's eyes were locked on Patty, her head tilted to the side.

Crapsnackles. I hadn't considered the whole German Shepherd and werewolf thing. I mean, a shepherd was pretty dang close to a wolf, weren't they? Hopefully, this wouldn't turn out to be a problem.

"Who's your new friend?" Patty asked calmly.

Okay, calm was good. And no visible teeth or growling from either of them. That was good, too.

"This is Jesse," Trevor said. Then he looked down at Jesse. "And this is Patty Bluespring. She's our very close neighbor." He lowered his voice and leaned down closer to Jesse. "She's also my boss, so be cool around her, okay?"

The soul stare between dog and werewolf was still going strong. It was starting to worry me. Then Patty stood and walked over to Jesse, putting her hands on either side of Jesse's face. Finally, the stare ended, and she smiled up at us.

I could breathe again.

"Jesse and I won't have any problems," she said. Then she paused. "In fact, she's more than welcome to join me when I go for midnight runs. Might do her good to get some exercise for that leg of hers."

Trevor didn't look so sure about that. Patty grinned at him.

"Trust me, I know what the dog needs even more than you do. Yes, she needs love. And I know the two of you will give her plenty of that. But that leg needs to run. Her heart needs that, too. And I promise to take it easy on her. We'll go slow. To start anyway. Work our way up to a full lope."

Trevor looked over at me, then slowly nodded. "That should be okay. But give us a few days to see how she does, all right? I mean, they wouldn't even let us sign the adoption papers until we kept her overnight on a trial basis."

Patty chuckled. "I'm actually surprised they let you do that. Bet there were waivers to sign, huh?"

Oh yeah. Lots and lots of waivers.

I glanced behind Patty at the house. I couldn't see Destiny, but that didn't mean she wasn't watching. If I didn't make that introduction soon, I'd be the one in the doghouse tonight. Figuratively speaking, of course.

We didn't actually have a doghouse. Yet. Jesse, if the adoption went through like we hoped it would, would be family. Family didn't live outside in the elements with only a doghouse to protect them. Family lived in the main house. The main house that was warded seven ways to Sunday.

Still, figurative doghouse or real one, I didn't particularly want to be in it. Destiny had a way of holding on to grudges against what she thought were slights to her.

"I know you're here for a reason, Patty, and I'm not trying to downplay or delay that, but if I don't introduce Jesse to Destiny soon..."

Patty chuckled. If anyone would understand my rush to get our hopefully new family member into the house, it would be her. After all, her familiar was Destiny's sister. And yes, she had a touch of the Goddess in her too.

"Let's go then," she said.

I unlocked the door and held it open for the others while my eyes scanned the room for Destiny. The feline was sitting high on the back of the sofa in the living room, her eyes intent on the dog at Trevor's side.

Trevor bent down to release the leash, but I laid my hand over his. "I'd hold off on that for a bit."

His eyes met mine, then traveled over to Destiny on the sofa. "Good call."

As if by joint agreement, we all stopped just inside the front door. All the better to give us some time and space should things go south.

Luckily for us, they didn't.

However, if the length of the soul stare between Patty and Jesse had been long, it still didn't hold a candle to the stare between canine and feline. Their eyes locked in a heartbeat.

But there was no surge on the leash, no growl, and not a single other sign of aggression that I could see on Jesse's part. Destiny didn't seem all that amused. At least not at first.

Her little kitty-cat cackles were definitely raised. But she wasn't hissing or spitting, so I took that as a win. Truthfully? If I was staring down an animal that was about twenty times my size, my cackles would probably be raised too. It was a survival kind of thing.

Instinct.

I'm not sure how long we stood there, silent as the grave. It was probably not nearly as long as it felt like it was. But we all had a silent agreement.

The next move was up to Jesse and Destiny.

Finally, Jesse took the lead. Walking slowly, and still fully connected to the leash in Trevor's hand, she made her way to sit in front of the sofa directly in front of Destiny. Then she lifted one paw and placed it on the cushion in front of her.

I knew Destiny didn't miss much. She would have noticed the definite limp in the dog's gait. It still took her another minute to cautiously climb down from the back of the couch to sit beside Jesse's paw. Her tiny body was still tense, and I could tell she was ready to run at a second's notice should Jesse move toward her.

After a few seconds of just sitting there quietly beside the dog, she gently raised a paw to put on top of Jesse's.

If I didn't know any better, I'd have sworn the dog smiled.

"She's obviously been around cats before," Patty said. "Looks like they've got a budding friendship going already. You got lucky on that one."

She didn't have to tell me that. I walked over and put a hand on both animals' heads, and squatted down to be more on their level.

"Jesse, this is Destiny. I'm a witch, and she's my familiar, so she isn't like any other cat you've ever known. She's special." That should give me a few brownie points with my feline. Then I turned to Destiny. "And Destiny, this is Jesse. She's had a pretty rough time of it in the past, and Trevor is thinking of making her his familiar. So if you could be extra special nice to her, I'd really appreciate it."

I wouldn't have had to speak the words as Destiny and I shared a more intimate form of communication, but I thought it was important to allow everyone in on that little conversation. Especially Jesse.

Destiny's eyes raised to mine. "You adopted her?"

"The adoption isn't official yet. They wanted us to keep her overnight and introduce her to you first."

The cat gave a sniff. "Smart idea, that." She tilted her head, her paw still on Jesse's foot, then slowly nodded. "I think she needs us." That last part was softer, almost a whispering thought.

I always knew my cat was off the charts smart. But now I knew she was off the charts caring too.

It felt good.

If there had been any lingering doubts about adopting Jesse, they were gone at that point. Destiny informed me that she would be the logical one to show the newest family member around the house, so the two furry beasts set off on their own to explore.

Jesse made sure to check with Trevor before leaving his side, but with his approval and Destiny's insistence, eventually, she agreed. But I noticed more than once in the few minutes directly following their departure that the dog came back to check that we were still there.

Yeah, there were definite issues there. Hopefully, having Destiny around whenever both Trevor and I had to leave the house would help. Only time would tell that, though. I did notice that the check-ins grew further and further apart, so I was taking that as a good sign.

Enough so that I could finally deal with the other issue at hand. Patty.

"So, were you coming by with news... or just checking in?" I asked her.

"Kind of both." She paused as we got situated around our dining room table. "I wanted to know if you had any leads, first of all. But I do also have a bit of news of my own."

Trevor's brow rose. "Tell us your news, and then we'll catch you up on ours."

Sounded fair enough to me. I mean, there were two of us and only one of her. Then again, she was the one with the most at stake here, so that probably didn't mean a whole heck of a lot.

She leaned back in her chair, taking a sip of her water first. "Well, one thing has really been bothering me about this whole thing."

Only one? She must have seen my look for what it was, because she quickly clarified. "Okay, so there are a lot of things bothering me about this, but one thing keeps coming back to the front of my mind time and time again." She paused a second for another drink. "Why did the sheriff from Oak Hill call me in on this?"

I felt, rather than saw, Trevor's glance shift my way. "Yeah, we've been asking ourselves that same question," I told her.

She nodded. "I figured you would have. Well, thanks to Steve, I have a partial answer on that front, at any rate. About a week ago, there was a small jailbreak from his facility. The night of Parsons' death, the sheriff got a call—an anonymous tip—telling him where and when he could find the fugitive."

"Let me guess," Trevor said. "It wasn't local to Oak Hill, was it?"

"Nope. About an hour away. The sheriff staked the place out all night, so when the call came in about the body in the woods—another anonymous one, by the way—he made the decision to bring me in."

Something about that didn't sound quite right to me. "Is that the normal protocol? The man has a ton of deputies, doesn't he? Was he that afraid they would botch the job before he got there?" And if he was, then why were still working for him?

"No. It isn't normal." Patty looked away. "Steve had that same thought, so he outright asked the sheriff why he called me in."

"And?" Trevor asked.

She looked him in the eyes. "And he said the deputy that reported the call to him suggested it."

I leaned in. Okay, now we were getting somewhere. "Which deputy?"

Patty shrugged. "Don't know, and the sheriff isn't saying. He knows Steve and I have a history, so he told Steve to stay out of it and off the case. Might have been better off if he hadn't approached the man about it. We lost our inside man on this."

Well, crapsnackles. Looked like my to-do list just got a little longer. I'd be checking into some deputy backgrounds tomorrow for sure.

"I'm really hoping you can tell me the two of you have come up with more than I have," Patty said.

I nodded to Trevor. He knew everything I did, and he spoke law enforcement. He'd know how to phrase things.

"We think we have a lead on who was with Parsons at the time of his death," he said. "It's not a take it to the bank lead, but it's a place to start."

One of Patty's eyebrows shot up. "Do tell."

He shrugged. "Everyone in town knows that Parsons wasn't exactly faithful to his wife. At the time of his death, he was having two affairs that we know of. One of which I think we can pretty much rule out."

"And the other?"

Trevor hesitated. "No proof on that one yet, but we think he was seeing Glenda Klein. His boss's wife."

"Is there any reason you're leaning toward her?"

He took a deep breath. "Well, for starters, two people have mentioned the possibility to us so far. That says something right there. Maybe Parsons wasn't as discreet about his affairs as he thought he was."

"And for enders?"

Trevor was dragging this out. I was regretting letting him tell our news. So at that point, I butted in myself. "For enders, the woman left town very shortly after Parsons' body was found… if not before."

Patty's other eyebrow shot up. "And the Oak Hill sheriff hasn't brought her in for questioning yet?"

"Not that I'm aware of. According to Mr. Klein, she went to visit her mom. I haven't had the chance to track that contact information down yet."

"Why not call the wife's cell phone? Everyone has one these days, you know."

"Again according to Klein, she didn't take it with her. Left it on the dining room table." Trevor was back in charge.

"That doesn't sound good," Patty said.

"I know, but Klein said she was always going off and leaving it behind. If you think about it, and the woman was having an affair that she didn't want her husband finding out about, she might not have wanted the GPS tracking her every move."

Patty nodded. "Okay, so I hadn't thought about that. Makes it more plausible, anyway." She hesitated. "But chances are, the woman had a burner phone. If you could track that one down, the GPS might be of excellent use to us."

"I'll see if I can pull some strings and get a copy of Parsons' phone records. If she did have a burner, I'll just bet the man called it a time or two."

Patty stood and brushed out the slight wrinkles from her slacks. "Sounds like the two of you have been busy and have things well in hand." She looked over at both of us. "Thank you. I hate being put on the sidelines for this, even if I do understand the why of that."

"We'll do our best to keep you posted," I promised her. "And if you hear anything new on your end..."

"I'll let you know."

Destiny and Jesse walked back into the room just as Patty was leaving. The woman paused and looked back at Trevor. "Not that I see this happening, but if the two of you decide not to adopt Jesse here, I'd love a heads up." She smiled down at the dog. "It would be nice to have a running buddy. Funny that I haven't thought about that before."

"Can't see it coming to that," I said. Not with the current look of adoration on Destiny's face. "But if it does, you'll be the first to know."

Trevor hooked the leash up to Jesse's collar, and we walked Patty back to her place. I think, even unspoken as it was, we all wanted Jesse to know exactly where she lived. Even Destiny tagged along. Sans leash, of course.

"You really don't need that chain, you know," she told me. "Jesse isn't going anywhere."

I really, truly hoped she was right. But we still had to get the shelter to agree to the adoption to seal the deal.

CHAPTER 12

It's never a good feeling to wake up staring straight into a tiny little kitty's face. Destiny was sitting on my chest and her not-so-gentle pit-patting on my chest had woken me. To stare directly into her eyes. Disconcerting, that.

"We have a problem."

Crapsnackles. From bad feeling to worse feeling. "Is it Jesse?"

She gave a short nod. "Yes." She paused. Knowing my cat, that pause was for dramatic effect. Destiny was great at milking her moments. "Jesse can't fit through the cat door."

My tension faded, and I let my head fall back onto my pillow. "That's the problem? We need a bigger cat door?"

"Don't scoff. It's a big problem. You know dogs poop, too, right? And Jesse's poop won't be little like mine and Yorkie Doodles. Her poop is gonna be big. You don't want that inside, do you?" Her little nose curled up to make her point even clearer.

"No, we do not." The cat had a point.

The night before, we had decided that it would be prudent to show the shelter just how serious we were about Jesse, so we'd made a second trip into town to select a fence. No chain link for me. Dang it all, I wanted a white picket fence. It was the only thing that would go with our perfect little Cape Cod house.

By the time we'd picked it all out and arranged to have it set up with a local handyman, it had been late. Jesse's nightly walk hadn't been all that long. By now, the poor dog was probably bursting at the seams.

I reached over to punch Trevor and get him going, but my closed fist hit empty space. He wasn't there. Only then did I glance over at the corner where we'd set up Jesse's bed. It was empty too.

I glared at Destiny. "Let me guess. Trevor and Jesse are already out on a walk, aren't they?"

Destiny licked a paw. "That would be correct, yes."

"And Jesse didn't have an accident last night that needs to be cleaned up, did she?"

"She did not." She seemed a bit affronted that I would ask, even though she was the one that had started that entire conversation about pooping indoors. That was my kitten, all right.

I picked her up off my chest and set her to the side. All that meant was that Destiny had absolutely no reason to wake me up in the manner that she had. She had probably figured it out to pay me back for some assumed slight I had done to her. Not that I had a clue what that slight was, mind you.

I had half a mind to roll over and go back to sleep. But chances were good that wouldn't last long. It couldn't take that long for Jesse to do her business. Besides, I had a lot of work to do today. Fitting in a new pet with an important investigation wasn't going to be an easy thing.

But first things first. A good witch always made time for her familiar. And if Destiny was feeling slighted, it would behoove me to find out exactly what I'd done and try to appease her. There were worse things than waking up into a kitty-cat soul stare. Trust me on that one.

"For the record, we're already on that. We looked at doggy doors last night at the hardware store, but we didn't want to order one until we get the adoption paperwork finalized." It would be too much of a bad memory if things didn't go well with the shelter.

I sat up and pulled Destiny over onto my lap. "So why don't you tell me what's really going on in that little kitten head of yours?" I softened the words with a long scratch under her chin.

She leaned into it and was silent for a minute. Most likely not wanting to risk a shortened scratch. Finally, she looked up at me. "Most families would discuss a possible pet adoption with everyone concerned before just doing it."

Ah, so that was it. I guess I should have known that. I'd gone and hurt her little feline feelings by not discussing Jesse before I'd brought her home.

This could be tricky.

"The adoption isn't a sure thing, Destiny. Last night was just a trial. To see how you and Jesse got along." Thank you, Mr. Lee, for saving my butt on this one. "And we would have discussed it with you, for sure, if it hadn't been such a spur of the moment thing. But after we met Jesse at the shelter... well, turned out neither of us felt right about just leaving her there."

I could feel some of the tension drain out of Destiny. "I guess I get that. Did they at least treat her right there?" She flexed her claws as she asked.

Better to nip that in the bud right now. I didn't want to give Mr. Lee the impression that we had psycho animals here.

"It's a shelter, Jesse, not a home. They do what they can to make the animals comfortable, and they were working with Jesse to try to help her limp get better, so there is that too. But there's only so much they can do to make the animals really feel loved."

She laid her head down on her paws, taking in a deep breath. "Too bad we can't adopt them all."

I had to agree with that one. But then we'd become a shelter ourselves, and things wouldn't turn out all that different for them. But there was something we could do to help them, surely.

"You know, we might be able to make it seem a little homier for the animals," I said, thinking my way through the words.

Destiny's ears perked up. "How?"

"Well, we could buy a few cat trees and toys for the feline enclosure. And maybe some dog beds and treats for the canines. Some toys for all of them, too."

Destiny hopped down onto the floor and then looked up at me. "Well, what are you waiting for? We have some shopping to do."

Um. We?

Turns out, *we* was the right word, after all. At Destiny's insistence, there were four passengers in Trevor's SUV when we left less than an hour later. Trevor at the wheel, me riding shotgun (as was my right), and the two new best furry buds in the back seat.

As anxious as Destiny was to go to the pet store, I put my foot down. There was one place we desperately needed to go first. My mothers. I'd already called ahead, and she was waiting for us.

There was a huge reason why that visit was the most important one on our daily task list. We had no guarantee that the shelter would allow us to adopt Jesse, and this might be our one shot at getting her some magical healing for that leg of hers.

Doctors could only do so much with the tools they had at hand. Mom could do more. Lots more.

It turned out that Mom being closer to Oak Hill than to Wind's Crossing was a good thing. Not only did that put us closer to a much bigger and better stocked pet store, but it also gave me time to do a little work on the investigation. Trevor being the one at the wheel helped on that last one.

I'd given up on trying to locate Mrs. Klein. Well, in a way, anyway. But her husband had said she was with her mother. And her mother was much easier to trace and track down contact information for. I hoped a phone call would work, because it would take over an hour's drive time for an in-person visit.

Time was a premium at the moment. I was feeling the stress of everything weighing heavily on me. Trevor and I had a lot of irons in the fire right now. Important irons. His journey into witchcraft, Patty's investigation, the Commissioner's hearing coming up, and now dealing with poor Jesse.

Good thing I was a powerful witch with a team behind me, huh?

I hadn't really expected Mrs. Jade (Glenda's mother) to answer at her house's landline. After all, she and her daughter were supposedly on a trip, weren't they?

As it turned out, no. They weren't.

"No, Glenda isn't here right now." The woman paused. "Did you have reason to think she would be? Have you tried to reach her at home?"

"We talked with her husband. He's the one who said she was with you. I'd have called her cellphone, but apparently, she left it behind when she left."

Mrs. Jade chuckled. "Well, yes, she was bad about that."

Something about that chuckle made me think the woman was fully up to date on her daughter's wanton ways. And more than that. It made me think that she fully supported her in those ways. What kind of family were we dealing with here?

"I'm guessing you knew about Glenda and John Parsons?" I held my breath. It might have been a small leap of faith on my part, but it was a leap none the less.

Another chuckle. "Oh yes. And I know this might not sound all that respectful to you, but I am behind her on that one hundred percent. That Klein man was never good enough for my daughter. To make her work in that dusty office... it just wasn't right. Breathing in all that dust day in and day out. It can't be good for a person, now can it?"

I wondered how to phrase the next question. In the end, I followed my normal mode and just flat-out asked it. "You do know that Parsons was married, too, right?"

She grunted. "For now. Glenda and John have both been to see a lawyer. He was going to give them a special deal and handle both of their divorces for a cut-rate price. A bargain, actually." Then she paused. "I hope that you keep that a secret until it's announced. We really don't want Klein to have any more warning than the necessary paperwork gives him."

It finally hit me. The woman didn't know that Parsons was dead. I had kind of wondered why Mrs. Jade was being so open with me. That probably wouldn't have been the case had she known I was calling looking for her daughter after the death of her lover.

I looked over at Trevor. He shrugged, leaving it up to me. Taking a deep breath, I just spilled the beans. "I must admit, I thought you knew, but I'm guessing now that you don't. John Parsons... has died, Mrs. Jade. And his body was found in very, well, odd circumstances. I'm truly surprised you didn't read about it in the paper or see it on the news."

There was a long moment of silence.

"Mrs. Jade?"

Her voice was much weaker when she answered. "I avoid the news. It only depresses me." Another silence. "John's really dead?" Then the timing of my call must have finally dawned on her. "You're looking for my daughter because you think she has something to do with that? Was he... murdered?"

Whoa, boy. How did I answer that one? The scene I was at with the man's body had definitely looked like murder. It had been meant to. It was only through the coroner's report that I supposedly didn't have access to that we'd learned about the heart attack and body moving thing.

"I really can't say any more than that the police are involved." I paused, sensing that the call was about to be summarily ended. "For the record, I don't think Glenda had anything to do with his death. But I really need to talk to her. I'll admit that her taking off on the night he was found dead doesn't look good for her."

"No. It wouldn't. When was that exactly?"

I gave her the date, and once again, the silence grew. When she finally spoke again, her voice had a definite steely tone to it.

"The one you want to be talking to is Klein. That date is the day that Glenda and John went to see that lawyer. Sounds to me like Klein found out. That man is more than a little cuckoo." She hesitated. "I'm coming to Wind's Crossing. I have to find my daughter."

"Actually, I'm trying to do that, and I have a lot of resources that you may not have access to. Can you tell me when you last spoke to her?"

"Right after they got done at the lawyer's office that day. They were supposed to be coming over to dinner on Sunday to celebrate." Her voice wavered. "I was fixing a pot roast with all the trimmings. Glenda's favorite."

"I know I've just given you a ton of things to think and worry about, but I do have one more question for you. Then I'll let you go, I promise," I told her. "If Glenda had needed to get away—for her own safety—where would she have gone?"

"Here." A definite waver this time. "She would have come here."

Crapsnackles.

CHAPTER 13

Even as I disconnected the call, I could feel the weight of Trevor's stare on me. I glanced over to find his eyes filled with worry and a touch of sadness.

"We need to have another talk with Klein sooner rather than later, don't we?"

Well, yeah, we did. Before that phone call, the whole missing wife thing was more of an implication of guilt. Now, the timing of her going missing seemed much more ominous. Especially if the whole story about the lawyer was a true one. And for some reason, I was kind of betting it was.

Kind of hard to lie about getting a divorce when you visit the lawyer with the woman you're leaving your wife for, isn't it?

My glance then went to the backseat, only to find two more sets of worried and sad eyes locked on me. Destiny, for sure, knew what was going on. Jesse was most likely just reading the feelings of the others in the vehicle. Poor girl. There was so very much on the line for her right now.

For us, too.

I took a deep breath. It was a hard call to make, but I was making it. "I say we continue on with this morning's activities as we had planned. Once we get the adoption paperwork signed and sealed, then we can visit the limestone mill again and have another conversation with Klein."

Trevor's eyes were back on the road. Safer for all of us that way. "It might sound selfish. Shoot, I know it sounds selfish, but that's my vote too. I don't want to give Mr. Lee any reason to not sign those papers. And we agreed to be there this morning to do just that."

"For the record, not that you would think to include me in the vote, mind you, but that's my choice too," Destiny piped in. She scooted a little closer to Jesse, too.

It was so sweet, I felt my heart swell the tiniest of bits. I just wished we'd had the time to introduce Jesse to Yorkie Doodle before taking this next step. But then, Yorkie loved everything and everyone, so I really didn't see an issue.

He might have been a touch jealous of Jesse taking over so much of Destiny's attention, but with him being a father now, he wasn't spending all that much time at our place, anyway. I really thought we were good there.

"We have Destiny's vote, too," I said. "No way to get Jesse's take on this, but I think we're all unanimous on this one. We'll go double-time on the investigation once we get Jesse into the family."

He seemed relieved at my words, his shoulders dropping just a bit. "Good." He glanced in the rearview mirror at Destiny. "Thank you for being so understanding about all of this."

Trevor didn't say it, but I knew within reason he'd been afraid Destiny would have issues with our hopefully new family member. But with a sweet girl like Jesse, what was there not to love? Made me want to find her previous owner and spend a little time with them.

Time I really thought I'd enjoy a heck of a lot more than they would.

Mom's eyes lit up when she first saw Jesse, and the fact that little Destiny was right there walking alongside her didn't escape her notice, either. One eyebrow raised as she looked at me over the animals. "Besties already, huh?"

"Yup. After we're done here, we're going to the pet store to buy Jesse the biggest bone they have—courtesy of Destiny—and then pick up some stuff for the shelter, too."

Mom nodded. "Remind me before you leave. I want to chip in on that." Then she got down to business. It didn't take all that long. Well, her part of the healing, anyway. About half an hour later, she called it.

"The veterinarian that did her surgery did a good job. She's healing nicely." Mom gave the leg a last, gentle rub. "And I just gave the healing process a little boost." She looked over at me.

"If you could reinforce the spell every eight hours or so, it would work even better."

I nodded. "If I can, I will." That wouldn't be a problem if Jesse went home with us. If, however, Mr. Lee didn't give us his approval, it would be a little trickier. Not that I wouldn't still try.

From there, we finally made it to the pet store, where we completely filled the back of Trevor's SUV. We left the dog beds off our list, for now anyway. I wanted to see what they were using for the dogs currently and get some input from Mr. Lee on those before I spent that kind of money. Even if, with Mom's donation to the cause, I was pretty sure we had enough to buy a comfy bed for every canine they had at the facility.

When we parked out front, Trevor looked over at me and then back at the back of the stuffed vehicle. "He's going to think we're trying to bribe him, isn't he?"

That same thought had crossed my mind. "Would that be such a bad thing?"

Trevor thought about it for a minute. "You know, I think it could be. Mr. Lee seems to be a stand-up kind of guy."

The man had a point. "So, how do we do this?"

He shrugged. "We go in, get the adoption in the bag, and then we make the donation? As a thank you rather than a bribe."

Sounded good to me. It wasn't like we were going in with empty hands. I'd been snapping pictures like crazy of the two furry besties, and we had a record of the fence purchase and the name and number of the handyman we'd hired to put it up, too. That should show the man just how badly we wanted Jesse to become part of our family.

It did. His hesitation was mostly for show, I thought. He looked from the pictures of Jesse and Destiny to the order for the fencing and back again with a smile on his face. "You all have been very busy."

Well, yeah. And he didn't even know the half of it.

Within half an hour we were all signed, and it was official. Jesse, for better or worse, was a part of the new Ravenswind slash Taylor family. No, I hadn't changed my name when we'd gotten married. Luckily, Trevor understood just how much the Ravenswind name meant to me. It was who I was. Getting married didn't change that. It just added to it.

As we stood and the two men reached over the desk to shake hands, Trevor gave him a huge grin. "Do you have a few minutes to spare? We have something for the shelter in the back of my SUV, and another pair of hands could come in handy."

Lee looked puzzled, but he nodded. That's all we needed. He followed us out and his eyes widened when Trevor popped the hatch up on his vehicle.

"All that is for us?"

"Yup," Trevor said. "Our way of saying thank you."

I waited until we had the haul all loaded up into the shelter's storage room. The pitiful state of their stores before our donation made me think this just might become a monthly thing for us. Between Trevor and me, we made more than enough money to run our household. Might as well give a little to a place in need that helped those unable to help themselves.

Once all that was done, I pulled out the envelope from my mom. "If you think that will help the shelter, then this might help even more."

Mom had given us cash to be used for the supplies as well as a check for the shelter. A very generous check. And every cent of what she gave us was in that envelope. The supplies were on Trevor and me... and Destiny, of course.

When Lee took a peek inside, he almost went down. Instead, he ended up leaning heavily on the receptionist's counter. "Oh, my goodness. You don't know what this means to us. We've been...." His words trailed off, and he shook his head. "No-kill shelters aren't cheap to run. We're always on the verge of going under." He hefted the envelope and smiled. "This will save a lot of lives. Thank you."

"Thank my mom, that's from her."

Credit belonged where credit was due.

After getting Jesse settled into the backseat again, and watching Destiny cuddle up for the ride, I turned to Trevor.

"So, where to from here?"

It was a good question. The limestone mill was just outside Wind's Crossing. Not even a five-minute drive from where we were at the moment. But there was a small issue. Well, technically, one small issue and one rather large one. Both sitting in our backseat.

I really didn't think it would set such a good precedent to take our animals into an interview with us. Kind of non-professional, I thought.

When Trevor didn't answer me immediately, I continued. "We should probably drop the animals off back home and then double back to the mill, huh?"

I got a little worried when he still hesitated.

Just as I was about to break and ask him what the heck was going on, he finally spoke. "I don't think I should leave Jesse alone this soon." He turned to face me, his eyes serious. "We can kind of guess that she has a history of abuse, and she probably has abandonment issues, too. I don't want her to think that's going to happen with us."

"Excuse me," Destiny said, her hackles rising. "She wouldn't exactly be alone, now would she?"

I motioned for Destiny to tone it down, as I was pretty sure that all Trevor could hear in that was an incessant kitty-cat whine. "Just for the record," I told him. "Destiny has pointed out that Jesse wouldn't be alone. I thought you should know that."

He glanced from me to my familiar and back again. "Duly noted. No offense to Destiny, but I'm not sure that a feline companion would be of as much comfort to Jesse as one of us would be."

Destiny's hackles rose even more. I cut her off. "For the record, Destiny, I'm siding with Trevor on this one. You are going to make a splendid companion for Jesse, but right now, I think she needs a little more assurance than that. Cats can't really take care of dogs, you know." Thinking quick, I added. "For instance, what would you do if Jesse needed to go to the bathroom?"

She licked a paw and started smoothing her rifled fur down. "Okay, so I'll give you that one. As long as you acknowledge my point."

"Your point has been acknowledged and duly noted, as Trevor said." That taken care of, I turned back to Trevor. "But I'm not so sure it's a good idea to take Jesse with us on an investigation."

He opened his mouth, but I held up a hand. "Not done talking yet. In the future, once we know how she reacts to different situations, then it might be a grand idea to have her tagging along. But we've only known her for about twenty-four hours at this point. What if loud noises set her off?" That limestone mill was not a quiet operation. "As you said, we don't know her history. I'm not sure we should start including her in our work until we get a better handle on her."

I could tell he wasn't too happy about it, but he nodded all the same. He knew I was right. "So, where does that leave us? You sit in the car while I go in and talk with Mr. Klein?"

Yeah, no. That wasn't going to happen. Besides, there was one other item to consider. One that I'd almost forgotten about.

"Isn't the handyman supposed to drop by today to start on the fence? We told him we'd be home any time after two. We need to show him the layout we want." A glance at the clock showed we still had time to make that. But only barely. "Here's the new plan. You drive us all home, and I help you get Destiny and Jesse settled inside. Then I hop in my little bug and drive back to the mill to talk with Klein. Win-win and that will cover all the bases."

He started the car, but the hesitation was still there. "I'm not sure I feel comfortable sending you in to talk with Klein by yourself. What if Glenda's mom's implication was right? What if Klein has done something to her?"

I cocked an eyebrow at him. "Are you questioning my ability to take care of myself?"

"Well, um, no—of course not. It's just that I..." His words trailed off. Yeah, they really didn't have anywhere else to go, did they?

I cocked the other eyebrow and wiggled my fingers at him. We both knew that, of the two of us, I was by far the one most packed with sheer firepower. Not discounting my mate here at all. Trevor could handle himself just fine without magic.

So could I, for the record. But with the magic? Yeah. Just try and stop me.

His shoulders slumped as he put the car into gear with a glance back at Jesse. "You see what I've been up against, girl? Between Amie and her familiar, I never win. I'm counting on you to even the odds a little. You'll have my back, right?"

Jesse chuffed right on cue.

She was so a part of our family now.

CHAPTER 14

Everything went right along with our new plan. By two-thirty that afternoon, I was pulling into the visitor parking spot right next to Klein's black as night Jeep. Good. That was kind of proof that I'd caught the man still there.

I skipped the whole ringing into the office thing, not wanting to give him the opportunity to say no. And possibly lock the door before I made it to him. This conversation wouldn't go the way of the last one. This time, I knew the lies and knew the right questions to ask. It made a difference.

His eyes widened when I walked into his office. They widened even further when I shut the door behind me.

Klein looked from the closed door back to me. "Now really isn't a good time."

"Too bad. If you hadn't wanted to see me again, then maybe you should have started by telling us the truth the first time."

Here's the thing. This was Wind's Crossing, and I was a Ravenswind. That last name meant a lot in our small town. The people knew who and what we were. Some of them might not want to admit the kind of power we truly had, but deep down, they knew we had it.

And my Aunt Opal's karma spells were legendary around here. No one wanted one of those thrown at them. Even the nicest of people had a skeleton or two in their closet that they were afraid might come back to bite them on their heinies. Karma spells were fantastic at helping those skeletons get their chance to do just that.

He glanced at the clock. "I'll give you ten minutes."

"Fine. Answer my questions with the truth, and that should be more than enough time."

Klein closed his eyes and leaned back. "So ask already."

"Why did you lie to us about your wife going on a trip with her mother? For the record, before you answer, I've spoken to Glenda's mom. Learned a lot of really interesting things, too."

He swallowed. "No doubt. That woman never did like me. Doesn't think I'm good enough for her precious princess."

"So where is she?"

Klein shrugged. "I don't know." He held up a hand to stop me from saying anything. "That's the God's honest truth, whether you want to believe it or not." He paused. "I'm going to go out on a limb and assume that Mrs. Jade told you about Glenda and John."

He grunted. "Funny thing that. An honest man making a dang fine living isn't good enough for Glenda, but a two-timing moron like Parsons was? Those women had their sights on the

Governor's mansion, and they thought Parsons would get them there. How sad is that? When love boils down to politics?"

Personally, I agreed with the man. Especially considering that I knew Parsons wasn't just a two-timer. He was a three-timer at the very least.

"Did you know Glenda was filing for divorce?" I tried to keep my tone neutral, but I must have failed at that. Either that or Klein wised up to the direction of my questioning and realized that my new information was putting him in the hot seat as a prime suspect in not only Parsons' death (which had not yet been announced as natural causes) but also in the disappearing act of his wife.

He clamped up. Hard. "We're done here. If the law has questions for me, fine. Then I'll answer them. But you aren't the law. I don't have to talk with you."

I shrugged and pulled out my phone. "Fine by me. I'll just give the good sheriff of Wind's Crossing a call and invite her to join us, then. Of course, she's a busy person, so she'll likely just send a deputy to take you to her instead." I tapped my chin. "Wonder how that will look to your workers?"

It was an empty bluff at best, as Patty had been told distinctly to stay off this case. But then, he didn't know that, did he? At least, I hoped he didn't.

We stared at each other over the desk for a solid minute. My aunt is the queen of staring contests, but I was next in line. A princess of staring, that was me. He lost.

Klein ran a hand through his hair and slunk down in his chair, a seemingly beaten man. "All right. Yes, I knew she was planning to file for a divorce. But she hadn't yet. And this wasn't the first time she'd seen a lawyer, either. I don't suppose her mom told you that, though, did she? We always worked it out in the end."

"How did you find out?" And perhaps more importantly, how did he know the papers hadn't been filed? That sounded like insider information to me.

I was right.

He closed his eyes again. "Lisa Parsons called me. Seems she has a second cousin—a close one from the sound of it—that works in the attorney's office. She called her to let her know what was going on."

I fought hard to keep my expression neutral, but it was a losing battle at best. "Mrs. Parsons knew about the visit to the attorney?"

Klein nodded and grimaced. "You bet she did. She was in a right tizzy when she called me, too. Telling me to keep my 'slut of a wife' at home, where she belonged. Like this all boiled down to my fault. If she couldn't keep her husband at home, then what chance did I have keeping Glenda there? It takes two to tango, as they say."

A lot of thoughts were racing through my brain at that moment. But the prime one seemed to be the importance of finding Glenda Klein. A lot rested on doing that. If the woman was okay, then she would be the one in a position to answer a heck of a lot of questions. If she wasn't okay—all right, if she were dead—then things really didn't look good for the man sitting across from me.

"Your wife had an office here, didn't she?"

He blinked at me. "What does that have to do with anything?"

"You want to find your wife? I can help with that. But I need something with her DNA on it. Chances are I'd find it in her office." The request made, I watched him closer than a hawk watches a rabbit hole.

It rather surprised me when he immediately stood. "Follow me. I'll take you there."

A quick walk across a paved driveway, and we were entering the second building of offices. The two offices on the bottom floor had signs on their doors that said Drafting. Not being familiar with the industry, I wasn't entirely sure what that meant. Not that it really mattered to me.

Our destination was the huge office at the top of the stairs. You could have fit four of Klein's offices in there and still had room to spare. Yes, there was dust, but there was also an abundance of very nice office furniture, including a large oak desk, executive office chair, and—was that a treadmill in the corner? Dang. I thought my office was nice... but this one was gorgeous.

Kind of made up for the thin coating of dust, if you asked me.

I glanced at Klein, then walked over to the huge desk. "What I need would probably be inside one of her drawers. You okay with me looking?"

He swallowed but nodded. "I want Glenda home to talk about this, so yes. If you can help make that happen, then I'm more than okay with it."

I was starting to feel like, just maybe, Klein wasn't the bad guy here. But it was far too early to make that call.

The first two drawers didn't help me much, but on the third, I struck the jackpot. There was an ashtray full of lipstick-stained cigarette butts. That would have done the trick, but then my hands would have smelled of nicotine for days. I'd much rather use the hair from the hairbrush beside it.

From its close quarters with the ashtray, there was still a slight, lingering odor, but nothing like having to use the source of the odor itself. I lifted the hairbrush from the drawer and held it up for Klein to see.

"May I take this?"

He hesitated a fraction of a second before nodding. "All those stories about you and your family. They're true, aren't they?"

My smile was a bit on the rueful side, I'm sure. "Not all of them, no. We don't eat children or sacrifice animals under the full moon. And we sure as heck don't worship the devil. But some of them, yeah. Some of them they get right."

"You can really cast a spell to find Glenda from the hair on that brush?"

"I can." And I would have done just that, too, had we not been interrupted by the ringing of not just one phone, but two. His office phone went off a scant second after my cellphone started its chirping. I knew the caller from that chirp.

Patty. I had to take this.

"Excuse me," I said, walking over to stand closer to the tread-mill in the corner. It wasn't exactly private, but at least he'd only be able to hear one side of the conversation. Mine. And I could watch what I said, now couldn't I?

"Amie here," I said. I really didn't want to give the man information on the caller's identity. That didn't seem wise, things being what they were.

"Hey, Amie. Remember you telling me about Glenda Klein and her mysterious disappearance?"

"I do. I'm at the limestone mill as we speak."

There was a slight pause. "You're with Klein right now?"

"That would be a yes." I turned to where I could keep him in my peripheral vision. "Is that important?"

"Could be. We've got a call in to the man now, and if at all possible, I'd love for you to see his reaction when he takes it."

The office's phone beeped and the system's intercom kicked in. "Mr. Klein, you have a call on line two. Mr. Klein, line two."

Patty must have heard it in the background of our conversation because she said. "That would be it."

"Wanna give me a head's up?" I asked as Klein made his way to pick up the phone on Glenda's desk.

"We just found Glenda Klein's body."

CHAPTER 15

For what it's worth, Klein didn't take the call well. At all.

It's kind of sad to see a grown man cry, but that's what the man did, all the same. I'd hung up from Patty so I could catch his side of the conversation. He had started by desperately trying to tell the officer on the phone that there had to be some kind of mistake. Denial.

When that didn't work, the tears had started. The officer must have asked to speak to me in the end, because he made a motion for me to come and take the phone.

I did. "Amie Ravenswind here."

"Hey, Amie. Patty again. I thought it would be more prudent to give you the directions rather than Mr. Klein. He doesn't sound like he's in a very good place right now."

"He isn't."

Patty paused, then asked in a low voice. "You think it's an act of some kind?"

"No. No, I don't." Few men can cry like that on demand. Not a sniffle here and there. The man was outright bawling by now. I didn't think that would be the case if he had known that call was going to come sooner or later.

He'd have had time to prepare himself for it. Wouldn't he?

I took down the directions to the crime scene and hung up. At Patty's request, I was to accompany Klein there. According to her, I wasn't supposed to make it a request either. If he refused, I was to call her back to send a deputy over.

First impressions of innocence disregarding, the man was still our prime suspect in this. As such, I really didn't think he should be leaving a person of authority's sight until Patty had some hard answers.

Not that I was a person of any kind of authority. I wasn't. But Patty trusted me, and for now, that was enough.

I reached down and touched the man's shoulder. He turned tear-drenched eyes up at me.

"It's really true, isn't it? Glenda's... gone?"

I nodded. "I'm afraid so." Mentioning the fact that she'd probably met her fate around the time that Parsons had met his would have just seemed like kicking a man when he was down. So I keep quiet about that part of it. The facts would work their way into his brain pretty soon, all on their own.

"Patty asked me to drive you to her." Then I just waited. If I'd been looking for an argument from the man, well, I didn't get it.

He just nodded and reached for some tissues from the box on his wife's desk. "Can you give me just a minute?" He blew his nose and then stood, squaring his shoulders. "I'll need to let my foreman know I'm leaving early."

"I'm parked next to you. I'll just meet you at my car."

There wasn't any harm in letting the man tend to business. There was only one way out of the mill's parking lot, and I would be between him and the exit. So it wasn't like he could sneak out past me and be in the wind.

Wasn't going to happen.

But the slight delay gave me a much-needed chance to make a quick call to Trevor. The man deserved a catch-up. It did rather surprise me when he asked for the directions to the farm where she'd been found, though.

I started to ask if he'd be coming alone or with Jesse, but Klein came out of the mill just as I was finishing with the directions. I'd find out soon enough, anyway.

Klein settled into my passenger seat and got buckled in as I started the car. "Thank you for driving me. I'm not sure I'd be safe behind the wheel right now."

"No problem." If the man wanted to think I was doing this as a favor, it was no skin off my teeth. In fact, maybe it helped the situation a bit. Put me on the man's side by his way of thinking. That couldn't be a bad thing, could it?

The farm in question wasn't far from the mill. A five-minute drive. I could have used the time to push Klein for more information, but then again, I wasn't quite that big of a jerk. The man needed time to pull himself together for what he was about to go through.

This would not be an easy thing for him. For any of us, really.

Patty hadn't gone into a lot of details about how the body had been found or where. Shoot. Now that I thought about it, she hadn't given me any details at all. Other than the fact that Glenda had been found. At least that meant they had a positive identification of the woman. That was something.

When I pulled onto the long dirt driveway leading to the farm, I didn't make it far before I saw Patty standing by the side of the road. I pulled over next to her.

"Park here rather than at the house," she told me. "It's closer."

She opened Klein's door for him and waited for him to get out. "Sorry to put you through this, Mr. Klein, but we want to get a good head start on finding out who did this. Our hope is that you can shine some light on that."

Klein once again squared his shoulders with only the slightest of sniffs. "Anything you need from me, just ask."

The man could be acting. I mean, technically, it was a possibility. But if he was? Then he'd missed his true calling. The performance would be worthy of an Oscar, at the very least.

"I was hoping you'd say that." Patty motioned with her hand, and a deputy joined us a scant heartbeat later. "William here will take your statement and then drive you home. The department will arrange to have your vehicle delivered to your house if need be."

He stood a little taller. "I want to see her."

Patty hesitated. "I'm afraid that isn't possible at the moment. We are still in the process of... recovering your wife's body."

Klein just stared at her. I could see the faint spark of hope flare into existence. "What? If you haven't recovered the body, then you can't be sure it's her, can you?"

The sheriff laid a gentle hand on his arm. "It's her, Mr. Klein. I wouldn't have called you had I not been totally sure of that fact. One of my deputies identified her. He says he knew her very well."

She looked at me over Klein's shoulder, and her eyes told me exactly what she meant by those words. Parsons hadn't been the only infidelity that Glenda Klein had been guilty of. That could turn out to be important. It wasn't only husbands who got jealous, now was it?

Crapsnackles, but that bothered me more than it should. As long as there is breath in my body, I just won't understand the rationale for breaking the vows of marriage. If the love dies, or a mistake was made, well, that's what divorce was created for, isn't it? You didn't just stay married and do your own thing, too.

That just wasn't right.

"I still want to see her."

Patty hesitated, then nodded. "It won't be for a while. But if you want to hang around until they get your wife in a better space for viewing, then I guess I can't see the harm in that. That said, you don't go anywhere near that scene until the deputy clears you. Got it?" Her tone had to let the man know she would not budge on that one.

He swallowed but nodded. "Okay."

The deputy took Klein over to one of the patrol cars in a line a little further down the drive, and Patty turned to me. "I probably made yet another mistake in having you bring the man here. But I didn't want the man left alone, and I couldn't really spare a deputy to go fetch him and play babysitter." She gave a slight headshake. "Plus, I wanted you and your camera out at that scene as soon as possible. You have a good eye for detail, and I think we're going to need that with the crime scene photos."

"I'll have to make do with my phone. My camera is at home."

Patty shrugged. "That'll work too. I trust you." She looked away, and I could tell she had more to say. I'll admit I was wondering what the devil she was doing out here talking with me and not at the crime scene helping them 'recover' the body. Whatever the heck that meant.

"Just spill it, already."

She took a deep breath. "Sorry. This is harder than I thought it would be." She still paused for a few more seconds. "I just turned in my badge to the senior officer at the site. I'm too close to this whole thing, Amie. Even if I didn't do this on my own, the commissioners would do it for me. Having me on this investigation is just muddying the waters. And no one needs that."

Double crapsnackles. I rather thought that meant that Trevor's vacation was going to be unceremoniously cut short. We'd already canceled the official honeymoon part of things, but I'd still hoped to fit in a little more time for the whole Witchcraft 101 thing. Didn't look like that was going to happen after all.

Not that I blamed Patty for that. I didn't. There wasn't anyone to blame for it... other than the killer in question, of course. And they'd be dealt with sooner rather than later if I had my say on that. But still, well, double crapsnackles all the same.

This wasn't exactly how I'd planned to spend the first week of my new married life with Trevor. Not even close.

"Just for the record, yes, I'm stepping fully back from the official investigation of both deaths. And I'm off the log as sheriff until those cases have been resolved in full. That isn't in question." Her eyes bore into mine. "That doesn't mean I don't want to be kept in the loop. Keep me updated, okay?"

This had to be eating her alive. Not being able to work on a case where someone had tried to implicate you would have to. It sure as heck was bothering me, and I wasn't the witch in question here.

"You can count on it."

She could count on me trying to put that to bed as soon as possible, too. I wanted her back on the job.

Commissioners be danged.

CHAPTER 16

I had another shock or two waiting for me once I reached the spot in question. It wasn't hard to find, even without Patty's help. The voices of men working led me to them.

The first shock was the 'senior officer' Patty had mentioned. Turns out, that senior officer was none other than Orville Taylor. I don't know how she managed that, but I was grateful that she had. Maybe I'd be able to keep Trevor on my side of the investigation after all. The unofficial one. And being investigating unofficially would work a lot better with Orville in charge of the official side of things.

That just went without saying. We were all on the same team. It's just that some of us weren't getting paid by county funds. Orville, at least, understood that.

He saw me coming and nodded toward the phone in my hand. "Take as many shots as you can. I have a feeling we're going to need all the photographic help we can get on this one. The evidence is going to be shaky at best, most likely."

I looked behind him at the men all milling around what appeared to be a hole in the ground. "It would help if I had some clue what I was taking pictures of. All Patty said was that you were having to recover the body. I'm still not sure what that means."

Orville took a deep breath. "It means whoever killed Glenda Klein never intended for us to find the body. Old man Cramer—the owner of this somewhat run-down farm-land—has been busted in the past for dumping trash into a sinkhole on his property. Anything you put down into a sink-hole tends to stay there. Unfortunately, it also does a dang good job of contaminating the groundwater system in the area. That makes it illegal."

I swallowed. I really didn't like where this was going. "They dumped her into a sinkhole?"

"They did. Or at least, they tried to. And if the body had made it all the way to the bottom of what Cramer says is a hole that seems to go down forever, most likely her body would never have been found. As it is, it got stuck on an outcropping of rock a few feet down."

"How was it found?"

Orville shrugged. "According to Cramer, he was taking a walk about his property, and he noticed that the metal lid the county had fit over the hole was slightly ajar. When he investigated, the smell came barreling out when the lid was lifted." Orville cleared his throat. "It doesn't take a genius to know that a wild animal wouldn't lift the lid, fall in, and then close it behind them. So, needless to say, that's when he called us in."

"I see. And about that us part..."

"I'm here as a favor. To Patty, the commissioners, and the county at large. It's been approved, so I'm official to be here."

"Never doubted that for a single second, Orville." I also never doubted for a second that while he was doing a favor for everyone he mentioned, he was also doing a huge one for other people, too. Namely, Trevor and I, the newlywed couple.

He jerked his head toward the milling men. "I've taken very rudimentary steps to make sure the body doesn't fall further into the hole, but beyond that, it hasn't been touched. We want the best photographic evidence we can get of the situation before we actually try to bring her up. If there is any evidence on the body, it could easily fall into the abyss at that time. I want a picture of it, at the very least."

I glanced at him and then down at my now dinky-seeming phone. It was a nice phone, but it had very limited capabilities as a camera.

Orville smiled at me. "I got your back. Patty mentioned that you probably wouldn't have your camera, so I put a call in to Trevor. He's on the way with your good one. For now, you can start taking shots of the area. Anything might end up helping. I trust your eye. And your instinct."

It didn't take long to capture what I could on my phone. Luckily, it also didn't take long for Trevor to get there with my camera bag, either. For the record, no, he didn't show up alone.

Jesse was with him.

Orville gave a grunt when he saw the dog at the end of the leash. "When did Wind's Crossing get a K-9 unit?"

I spared Jesse a look. Now that he put that thought into my head, I could see his reasoning for asking. Jesse was the model of an efficiently trained police dog. She was sitting patiently beside Trevor, and only moved when he did. At a crime scene with lots of people and scents to check out, that was the very epitome of good dog behavior.

That kind of behavior took training. And lots of it.

Trevor grinned at his dad. "They didn't. This is Jesse. She's the newest member of our little family." He glanced down at her and his grin slipped just a little. "She does seem to be pretty used to all this, though, doesn't she?"

Orville nodded. "I'd be checking into her background if I were you. But for now, just keep a steady hand on that leash. I don't need a free-agent dog ruining my crime scene."

"You got it. We'll stay on the edges just to be safe."

I left the two men to continue their conversation. Now that I had my proper equipment, I had important work to do.

Taking my time, I got images from every angle possible without actually lowering myself into the hole to get them. I drew the line there.

With the zoom capabilities of my camera, I really didn't think that level of commitment was necessary to the job at hand. As yet, I had seen nothing that could be classified as a clue. But then, that's what the images were for. Once taken and uploaded onto a computer, they could be zoomed in even further to check for the tiniest detail.

Sometimes, cases were closed all on the basis of a single photograph. And yes, some of those photographs had been taken by yours truly. A fact I was very proud of, thank you very much.

As I snapped away, one thought was rather persistent in my brain. If the intent had been for her body to fall down into the sinkhole, then why had the killer left the job only halfway done? After a few minutes of hard work with a long stick, I really thought I could get the job done myself.

If I could do it, why hadn't they?

By the time I gave the sheriff the nod to start the removal of the body, the question still hadn't resolved itself. So I sought out the one who might be best able to answer it. Farmer Cramer.

It wasn't hard to seek him out, as I found him on the sidelines talking with Trevor. The man rose in my estimation when I saw him occasionally reaching down to pet Jesse. He seemed to know all the right spots to scratch, too, from the canine's reaction to those pets of his. I'd be taking notes for sure.

After all, I'd never been around a large dog before. Not for any length of time, anyway.

I joined them, then gave them a minute to finish out their current topic of conversation. Trevor had his own line of questioning. A line that made perfect sense, too. It revolved around who knew about that sinkhole of his.

Unfortunately, come to find out, pretty much the entire county knew. He'd been busted by the county commissioners a couple of years back for the whole dumping trash down it thing, and it had made the local papers.

According to Cramer, he'd practically had to fight off teenage boys with a stick to keep them from trying to go down the hole to explore. Seems they were certain that sinkhole of his would lead to an entire cave system under his farmland.

And who knows? They could have been right about that. But Farmer Cramer didn't want the hassle of all that. And he sure as heck didn't want the liability risk of the kids' adventure time.

"For about a year after that story broke, I had to let my dogs roam the farm free at night." He took a second or two to spit to the side. "Then the neighbors started complaining about that, and I had to corral them again."

There was a thought. "Were they corralled the night the body was dumped?"

Cramer gave me a shrewd look, then he nodded slowly. "Well, first off, I cain't really answer that proper like, because I cain't say exactly when that happened. But I will say that a few nights ago, the dogs had a conniption fit. Barking and carrying on to beat the band. Not like them at all."

He paused to give Jesse an extra scratch under her chin. The dog leaned into it.

By now, Trevor must have got where I was going with my questions, because he joined in. "You let them loose, didn't you?"

Cramer hesitated, then nodded. "Ain't much sense in having dogs if you don't let them do their job and protect your property, now is there?"

"You didn't happen to go with them, did you?" I asked. I was fairly certain I knew the answer to that, but it was better to ask and be sure.

He just shook his head. "Middle of the night like that? Nah. Not when it was probably just some teenagers looking to scope out the sinkhole." He spat to the side again. "That'd have been a different story if I'd known what was really going on out there, now wouldn't it?"

Yeah, it probably would have been at that. I could see Farmer Cramer not being all that hard on adventure-seeking teenagers, but I really thought he'd draw the line at people using his property as a body-dumping ground.

Still, something about how the man was acting had my witch's intuition firing up on all cylinders. What could that be, I wondered?

"Were the dogs okay when they got back?" I watched him closely when I asked the question, so I clearly saw the slight narrowing of his eyes. Yup. Something there, all right.

He spat again, then scratched his chin. "Nothing wrong with any of my boys. Right as rain, they were."

I nodded. "Did they happen to bring anything back with them?"

Trevor was staring at me. Guess my witch's intuition was beating out his former-sheriff's intuition this time.

Cramer's eyes narrowed even further, then they looked over toward the sheriff and the men working around the sinkhole opening. He was silent for a good, long minute.

I waited. Sometimes people were more cooperative in the end if you didn't push them. I had a strong feeling that maybe Farmer Cramer was one of those types of people.

And I was right, too.

"Follow me," the man said. Then he took off walking.

With a backward glance at Orville and his team, we followed. Me, Trevor, and Jesse. It didn't really surprise me when we ended up at the farmhouse.

Cramer pointed to the floor of the porch. "Wait here."

It didn't take the man long. When he returned, he handed me a small swatch of brown fabric.

I looked from it back up at him. "And this is...?"

"The trophy my dogs brought back that night," he said. "Now I cain't say for certain where they got that, you know, so it weren't like I was withholding evidence or anything like that. Just for the record."

I handed Trevor the fabric, wondering if he'd make the same instant connection I had. That shade of brown was fairly distinctive to me.

If he made the connection, he didn't share it with me. Instead, he just took a plastic baggie out of his pocket and put the material into it. "How did you find this?" he asked.

Cramer hesitated. "Well, old Frank gave it to me personal like. Pretty proud of himself, too. That's what makes me think that just maybe it came from someone trespassing on my property. But again, I got no way to prove that's the case. Understand?"

Trevor nodded. He must have understood what Cramer was saying, even if I didn't. Unless it was the whole withholding evidence thing, I didn't have a clue on that one.

I looked Cramer dead in the eye. "Is there anything else, whether or not you can prove it has to do with that body out there or not, that you can tell us that might help? That woman deserves justice, and her husband deserves closure. Neither of them will get either of those things without your full cooperation."

Cramer nodded slowly. "That's it." Then he hesitated. "Well, there is one other thing."

"And that other thing is?" Trevor asked.

"I'm not all that sure how familiar you all are with my property's layout. There's an old dirt road that people use for 4 wheelers that runs pretty close to where that sinkhole is. Might be where they parked that night. Fairly certain my dogs would have noticed if they'd used my drive."

Cramer's eyes gazed into mine. "For the record, I want the killer caught, too." He spat one last time to the side, making sure, I noted, that it went off his porch. "I cain't abide by murder."

That was good to know.

Now that we had the full of Cramer's knowledge of that night's happenings, I wanted nothing more than to make it back to Orville and his crew.

I wanted to test out my working theory.

Because that little swatch of fabric now resting in Trevor's pocket sure looked like it had come from a sheriff or deputy sheriff's uniform to me.

Sheriff station brown. That's what that color should be called.

Because it was an exact match.

CHAPTER 17

Even with Farmer Cramer's explicit directions, the dirt road was not an easy one to find. That had to be an important fact, didn't it?

"Who would know about this road?" I asked Trevor. "I mean, besides the four-wheeling crowd." Or maybe we needed to take a closer look at the four-wheeler crowd in general. Could be a starting place, anyway.

He shrugged as he stopped the car dead center in the middle of the road. As this was a definite one-lane, one-way kind of road, he was effectively blocking the road by doing that.

"Could be any number of people. Ones that own four-wheelers and like to go mudding after a hard rain. Outdoorsy types that like to camp in primitive conditions. Or, heck, even Sunday drivers that take any path that's wide enough for a car to fit into." He hesitated. "Any number of people could know about it. That doesn't really limit our suspect pool at all."

Okay, so I got that. But still… "But if they knew about the road, then it could be yet another tiny little nail in their coffin of a defense, couldn't it?"

Trevor nodded. "That it could be." Another brief hesitation. "If it proves out this is where the killer parked his vehicle."

I glanced out the side window. Trees lined the narrow road on both sides, crowding in to the surface of the road itself. In fact, the road was bumpy in places from errant tree roots from said trees. There was only one good spot to pull a vehicle to the side anywhere near Cramer's farm.

We were currently sitting on the road right beside that spot. Trevor put the SUV in park and reached for his door handle.

"You're just going to leave the car blocking the road?"

"Yup. Anyone comes down this road, and I'd kind of like to have a little talk with them," he said. "Wouldn't you?"

Well, now that he said that, yeah, I kind of would.

We got out, and he signaled for Jesse to join us. Somewhere down the dog's history trail, there had to have been a lot of training involved. Most dogs wouldn't have waited for that signal. I also noticed that Trevor didn't use the leash this time.

I hoped he knew what he was doing. He was putting an awful lot of trust in a dog that we'd scarcely known for an entire day.

Before we even made it the few steps to the little pull-off clearing, Trevor nodded to the camera that was still around my neck. "Get that thing working before we get any closer. Otherwise, Dad is likely to have my head on a spike for ruining a possible lead trail."

Right. Like that was going to happen. Orville had trusted his son to follow him as the sheriff of Wind's Crossing. He would bloody well trust the man not to ruin a crime scene. Or a scene leading up to a crime scene, either.

I snapped pictures every step of the way. The pull-off was in fairly poor condition. The weather had been pretty dry lately, so there wasn't any sign of a parked vehicle having been there recently, but then I'm not even sure what sign there would be. It didn't really mean there wasn't, just that we couldn't prove there was.

What there was, however, was a bunch of little dig spots of torn-up grass and dirt. Not the kind that a vehicle would make, however.

"You make anything of this?" I asked him.

He just shook his head. "Nope. But if you're finished with the pictures, I'd like to give something a try."

"Try away."

Trevor knelt down beside Jesse and patted the earth. Jesse immediately sniffed the ground and if I didn't know better, I'd swear the dog nodded. Then Trevor made a motion and the time for thinking was over because Jesse took off like a bolt.

For a few seconds, I was afraid Trevor had overstepped in turning her loose. I mean, hadn't Orville said he didn't want a free-agent dog roaming around his crime scene? This could turn bad.

But it didn't. Just before Jesse went out of eyesight, she stopped and paused, looking back at us.

"Hold there," Trevor said.

She did, giving us time to catch up to her. I was looking at the dog with all new thoughts cropping up in my head. Could Orville have gotten that K-9 part of things right? But what department in their right mind would give up a great K-9 asset like Jesse?

I'd thought she'd paused just to allow us to catch up, but once we were standing beside her, I saw another reason. There was a definite mark in the grass. The kind of mark that someone dragging a body along behind them might make.

Trevor grunted. "Guess they got tired of carrying her at this point."

It was as good of a theory as any.

The drag marks went a few yards and then stopped again. "Must have gotten his wind back," I said.

Trevor shrugged. "Or realized he was leaving a trail. I really don't think they intended for Glenda's body to ever be found."

I didn't think so either. The only question in my mind was, why? If they were just trying to make Patty look bad, then why did Glenda have to die? And why, if they had gone to so much trouble to set up Parsons' death scene, had they decided to just ditch the body rather than do the same with her?

This time, we were definitely talking about murder. If they'd really wanted to incriminate Patty in a murder charge, this would have been the one to do that with. They had to have known that eventually, the coroner was going to come back with the cause of death for Parsons being a heart attack.

Didn't they?

Trevor brought out the leash at that point, and we went at a much slower pace. All the way to the blasted sinkhole area. And all following the good nose of our little Jesse.

Orville seemed a bit surprised to see us emerge from the woods behind him.

Less than an hour later, we were at Clucky's Chicken Palace for a nice supper meal. No way was I going to cook after a day like today.

It was a good thing that they had outside dining, too, because Jesse was still right there with us. And yes, she got chicken too. She'd bloody well earned the treat in my mind.

Patty was sitting across from us, looking through the images I'd taken from the day's investigation. When I noticed her frowning and pausing at an image, I broke.

"See something we missed?"

We'd already filled her in on everything we knew. So she was as up to date as we were on the situation. The images were filling in the little details.

She hesitated. "Maybe." Her teeth caught her bottom lip for a second. "You said the farmer set his dogs out after the trespasser, right?"

"That's what he said."

"Well, from this image here of the dirt road pull-off, I'd say that they chased the killer all the way back to his vehicle." She tapped the camera's screen lightly. "Dogs don't like losing their prey any more than we do. They might have dug at the ground here in frustration if he made it into his vehicle."

"But he didn't exactly get away Scot-free," I reminded her. "One of the dogs did bring back a little brown trophy."

"True," she said slowly. "Wish I could have seen that. You're sure it's a match for the brown of our uniforms?"

I nodded. "I am. But as Orville pointed out, lots of other clothes use that shade too. It doesn't mean it has to be someone from a department."

"No," she said. "It doesn't have to be." She paused. "But, you know, I'm still rather stuck on why I was called into that first crime scene to begin with. Wasn't it a deputy that suggested that?"

Crapsnackles. So it had been. "Yeah, but the sheriff wasn't very cooperative about giving us the name."

"Maybe it's time I paid the man a little visit in person," Trevor said. "Knowing what we know now, I'd say it's time for him to stop playing so coy with us."

I could tell that Patty had something to say. I could also tell she was trying to choose her words very carefully.

"It's just us, Patty," I told her. "Whatever you have to say, just say it."

She glanced over at Trevor with a slight grimace. "It's just that I think he would cooperate a lot more freely if it were Orville having the little in-person visit with him. I know the man admires Orville's history as sheriff. I don't think he'd hide anything from him."

She had a point. As Trevor worked under Patty, that could be a slight hiccup in getting the man to talk.

"You have a good point, Patty. I'll talk to Dad and have him make that call," Trevor said.

"Good." Patty was looking back at the image on the camera screen again. "I'm asking just to be safe, mind you, but Orville is checking with local doctors and hospitals for dog bite victims, isn't he?"

"He is," I said. "The calls are being made even as we speak."

She nodded slowly, her eyes still glued to the image before her. "You might want to expand those calls to local body shops." Finally, her gaze lifted to me.

"Cramer's dogs might have taken some of their frustration out on the killer's vehicle, too."

I smiled.

Now we were getting somewhere.

Part of me wanted to leave right then and get on the phone to auto body shops. Witch's intuition again, I thought. But Patty just might have a good thought there. And it would be important to get to the vehicle before they repaired it to have the best chances of proving what those scratches really were.

Not something to wait around on.

On the other hand, I was still hungry and Clucky's chicken buffet was really, really good. Besides, as much as I hated to admit it, the auto body shops were all likely to be closed this time of day, anyway. So those calls would have to wait until morning.

At least now it felt like the case was moving along in the right direction. I liked that feeling. A lot.

"Okay, so now that we've gotten the ultra-important case stuff out of the way," Trevor started. "Are you sure you made the right decision today, Patty? Turning your badge over to Dad?"

She took a deep breath but nodded. "Yes. I'm sure. Me being on the case with everything being what it is simply wasn't a good idea. And you can't bloody well have a sheriff not in an active role when there is a murder in their district. So yes, I made the right call."

"But once this is over and done with, and your name is cleared, you'll take the badge back, right?" I asked. I was really hoping the answer would be yes. Orville wouldn't be up to taking the job back full-time. We all knew that. The man had retired for a reason.

And I really didn't want to go back to having Trevor be the sheriff. It was bad enough being the partner, now wife, of a deputy. Sheriff's hours were far, far worse. Not to mention all the midnight calls and disturbed sleep.

But all that was really beside the point, anyway. The main point here, and I'd keep telling myself that, too, was that Patty Bluespring was pretty much the perfect sheriff. And she seemed to enjoy the job, too. That was important.

If ever there was a witch born to keep the peace, that witch was Patty.

The bad thing was, she was stalling on answering my question. That just couldn't be good news for any of us.

Finally, she shook her head. "I'm not sure where my path will lead from here, to be honest." She paused, looking away. "The Council has made it patently clear they would like me back in my old role as enforcer. That might be my best option at this point. No problem with me being a witch in that job. It's a job requirement."

"But is that what you want to do?" Trevor asked, his voice quiet.

Patty shrugged. "To be perfectly honest, I was pretty happy being the sheriff. I'm not in this line of work for my health. You know that as well as I do. I'm in this to help people, to protect them from all the bad people... and other things... out there. I thought maybe having a sheriff that knew the real score on how things stood in the world might make a difference for Wind's Crossing."

She took another deep breath. "I thought I could do more good here than with the Council. But if the people don't want a witch for the job, what can I do?"

I slapped my hand on the table. The others jumped. Yeah, usually I contained myself better than that, but it had been a long day.

"You can let the people decide what they want, for starters. Not just one or two or three people with illusions of grandeur because of their position on some stupid county council. The sheriff's position is an elected position. Last I knew, you won that last election fair and square. Sounds like the people weren't so against having a witch on the job after all to me. I mean, you've never once denied who or what you are, have you?" I hesitated. "Well, the witch part, anyway."

Patty blinked a couple of times, then a change slowly came over her. She was sitting a little taller in her chair, for one. And her eyes got that determined look in them again.

I liked that look a whole heck of a lot better than the lost one that had been in them just seconds before.

Badge or no badge, Sheriff Patty Bluespring was back on the job.

Chapter 18

There wasn't a lot more that we could do that night, so we all trailed back to our community property. Patty to her little cabin, and Trevor and I to our much bigger Cape Cod.

He was all for heading straight to bed, but I had other ideas. I totally understood the importance of our present case. I got that. But I also understood the importance of the first few days of being a witch.

That was important, too. It wouldn't do to just let life go on as it had before, making no effort whatsoever to draw Trevor more firmly into the Wiccan lifestyle.

Besides, the current situation fairly screamed for a meditation session if you asked me. What better way to clear our minds and prepare for a good and restful night's sleep? Not to mention the fact that every now and again, a good meditation session would free up some of the worrying thoughts and let a stray, important thread come to the light.

Those little miracles could really get a person hooked on the whole meditation thing. Just ask any witch. They happened more often than you'd think. Sometimes we just had to get out of our own dang way.

"Meditation?" Trevor asked, his voice a little higher than its usual deeper tone. "Now?"

I nodded. "Yes. Meditation. Now." I smiled at him, trying to ease him into it. "Right now, we both have a million and one things fighting for precedence in our brains. We need to clear our thoughts so that we can rest easier... and maybe find the one thing we've been missing."

If ever a person got a side-eye, I got one then. "Meditation does that?"

"It does. Plus, it's in the second chapter of that remedial training book of yours. If you want to be a witch..."

"All right, all right," he said, throwing up his hands. "How long do we have to chant for?"

I blinked at him. "Chant?"

He blinked back at me. "Don't you chant when you meditate?"

"Not as a rule, no." Boy, did he ever have a lot to learn. I'd have thought being around my family his whole life would have taught him better than this. "It's more just getting into a comfortable position and focusing on your breathing."

Some of the tension fell out of his shoulders. "Oh." Then he nodded. "Okay, I can do that."

We'd see. Most people thought they could meditate. They thought it was easy. As it happens, for some people, it was one of the hardest things on earth to master. Go figure. And the problem was, I was kind of betting that Trevor would be one of those people. I was hoping to be proven wrong on that count.

I had a lot riding on this one.

Lucky for Trevor, he wasn't going into his first-ever meditation attempt alone. He had me to talk him through it. Guided meditation was always far easier than just trying to wing it.

A half an hour later, I opened my eyes to find Trevor laid out on the floor, softly snoring. I grinned at him. Lightweight. Still, not bad for a first attempt. Especially after the day we'd both had.

I thought about throwing a blanket over him and just leaving him there, but I didn't. We weren't exactly kids anymore, and a night sleeping on a cold, hard floor would be murder on the man's back. And yes, a part of me was being selfish, too. I needed the man at his best for whatever tomorrow might bring, dang it all.

His eyes popped open as my hand hit his shoulder. "Crapsnapples," he said. "I fell asleep, didn't I?"

I nodded at him. "You did. But don't feel too bad. Most people fall asleep until they get the hang of it." Then I hesitated. "And by the way, it's crapsnackles, not crapsnapples."

He grinned at me. "For you maybe. For me, I kinda like crapsnapples."

What could I say? The man I'd married was a touch on the weird side. Just the way I liked them. Well, loved them in this particular case.

We walked up the stairs hand in hand. About halfway up, Trevor paused. "You know, I had a thought right before I fell asleep. Or maybe right after... I'm not totally sure about the timing."

I stopped and looked over at him. "What thought was that?"

"I was thinking that what we needed to do, if at all possible, would be find the primary crime scene."

"The primary crime scene?" I wasn't quite there yet.

"Yeah. You know, where the murder actually took place. And, just maybe, where Parsons had his heart attack, too. If we could find that, then maybe we could get some important questions answered. Like, for instance, why Glenda Klein had to die."

What can I say? Sometimes it takes a while for all the little details in my brain to line up and start the cogs all firing together to form a theory. It might have been the meditation, or it might have been Trevor's thought, but either way, the cogs were firing nicely now.

"Parsons' office," I said.

"Excuse me? What about Parsons' office?"

"I'll bet that's where the primary crime scene is. Parsons' office. Betty at the shelter said that he met with affairs there. Too cheap to get a motel room, plus the added privacy of not having to sign in, most likely. Anyway, didn't she say he was meeting with his other affair that night? They'd probably be celebrating talking to that attorney, wouldn't they?"

Now he was staring at me. And I had a funny feeling we were no longer on our way to bed.

I was right, too.

As luck would have it, we were on our way out the door when Patty was just stepping up onto our porch. She glanced at us, then down by Trevor's side at Jesse.

"I was hoping you all would still be up."

"Is everything okay?" I asked. "We were just on our way out to check up on a lead. Well, a theory anyway."

She opened her mouth, then closed it and shook her head. "I'd love to hear about the theory, but to be honest, right now, I just need a really good run." Patty reached out to pat Jesse's head. "I was kind of hoping I could borrow Jesse for company."

Trevor looked at me with a question in his eyes. I shrugged. Jesse was technically more his dog than she was mine.

"You think Jesse will handle the whole wolf thing okay?" he asked.

Patty chuckled. "She'll probably handle it just fine, but that's for another night to test out. I'll stay in skin for this run. I think she needs to get to know me as a human first. The wolf part can come later."

"You want her leash?" Trevor asked. His way of saying yes, I'd guess.

Patty smiled at him. "Not unless that's a requirement for me to take her with me. I don't think it'll be necessary." She bent down to look Jesse in the eyes. "Will it be, girl?"

She must have been satisfied with whatever non-verbal response she got from Jesse, because she straightened up and looked back at Trevor. "So, is that a yes?"

"That's a yes. Only..." His voice trailed off for a short pause. "I'm not sure how long we'll be gone. It could be a while, and I really don't want Jesse alone for the first few days at least. I want her to know that she's home."

"Good to hear. We'll make it a nice, long run, and then I'll take her to my place for a midnight snack. You can pick her up there when you're done with your... theory. Maybe I'll even be ready to hear about it by then."

Sounded good to us. Trevor and I got into his SUV and left. I thought I saw Destiny looking out at us through the front window as we left.

Lucky for me, she seemed to approve of the situation. I know it might not seem like it, but that was really good news to me. Making your familiar unhappy wasn't the way to go when one could at all avoid it.

Especially when your familiar was Destiny.

Trevor had insisted on calling his dad to meet us there, and what with the slight hold up on our front porch, and the fact that he just lived much closer than we did, Orville beat us there by a mile.

In fact, by the time we got there, there were a couple of cop cars sitting by the curb beside Opal's old Buick. I rather thought that might mean something important.

I was right on that one, too.

Orville was waiting for us in the hallway outside Parsons' office. "Good thought you two had about the office. We found traces of blood on the rug, and on the corner of a lamp on the desk. Whoever cleaned it up didn't do a thorough enough job of it."

"Anything else seem out of place?" Trevor asked, his eyes darting behind his dad and into the office.

"Not that we've noted so far. Just an ordinary office. No signs of struggle. If this was the primary crime scene, and for the record, I think it is, then whoever it was either caught Mrs. Klein by total surprise, or they did a better job cleaning up after themselves than I at first thought."

Orville looked back into the office. Two deputies were making their way systematically through the room. "The bad thing is, this is an office that is pretty much open to the public. Anything we find will have to be eliminated from the routine everyday stuff before we can count it as evidence."

That would make things more difficult, for sure.

"I'm trying to contain the scene as best I can at this late date, so I'd ask that the two of you do your looking from out here in the hall. Sorry. I know that might not sound fair, seeing as you're the reason we're here to begin with."

"Sounds fair to me, Dad. You have to do what you can with what you have," Trevor said. I just went with a nod of agreement. No argument out of me.

Of the three of us standing there in that hallway, Orville had—by far and away—the most experience with this sort of thing. If there was anything to be found in that office behind him, he'd bloody well find it.

With or without me and Trevor.

CHAPTER 19

Not knowing exactly how long a 'long run' was by Patty's standards, we took the liberty to stop off for a little snack on the way home. As we'd already stuffed ourselves at Clucky's Chicken Palace earlier, we went with a simple ice cream cone.

Well, Trevor's cone was simple. I ordered mine dipped in a hard chocolate coating. Yum.

By the time we made it back to our little estate, we found Patty and Jesse sitting on her tiny front porch. As she'd promised, they were having a little snack, too. Only their snack wasn't so little, nor nearly as sweet, as ours had been.

Their 'snack' was a freshly grilled steak. No sides, either. Just the meat. It had to be a wolf thing. Or, in Jesse's case, a dog thing.

But then again, German Shepherds and wolves were a lot alike, weren't they? In some cases, so much so that they were a bit hard to tell apart. I bet that went for the inside of them, too.

I mean, come on, isn't there a bit of a wild animal in all of us? Some of us just buried it a little deeper than others did. That's all.

"How did your theory turn out?" Patty asked, her plate now empty. That steak sure didn't last long. Jesse wolfed hers down too, but she didn't beat Patty by all that much.

"That depends," I said, watching her as she wiped the corners of her mouth with a napkin. "Are you sure you're ready to hear about it?"

Patty nodded. "More than sure." She laid a hand on Jesse's head and smiled. "That run did me a lot of good. It helped me get my head on straight again. I'm thinking maybe I acted a little too hasty in giving up my badge. I'm a dang good sheriff, darn it."

Trevor was grinning. Well, so was I, come to think of it. This was more the Patty I'd grown to love and respect.

"I'm pretty sure Dad would give it back, no questions asked," Trevor told her.

Patty nodded. "He would. But after we talked for a few minutes, we both agreed that I'd act as a secondary investigator. That should appease the public. I mean, after all those years Orville spent as their sheriff, if they can't trust him... who can they trust?"

"But you're back on the case?" Sue me, but I wanted a concrete yes on that one.

She smiled at me. "I'm back. Orville didn't have a lot of time to talk. He said you two would fill me in when you got home. So start filling, if you don't mind."

We did. A few minutes later, she was up to speed with everything we knew, and I was yawning. It was well past my bedtime by now, and my body was letting me know.

Trevor squeezed my hand. "Just a minute more and then I'll get you to bed, I promise." He turned back to Patty. "What's your plan for tomorrow?"

Her face set. "Orville and I are going to visit the Oak Hill sheriff's station. As a united front. That little brown piece of fabric and that deputy's recommendation to call me in on finding Parsons' body has me bugged more than a little."

Yeah, it did me too. But if Patty and Orville were handling that part of things, it left Trevor and me open for another path.

I glanced over at him. "You got plans for us tomorrow?" I mean, it was always polite to ask before just telling him what I wanted to do. Wasn't it?

He nodded. "I think we need to pay Lisa Parsons another visit."

Well, what did you know? We were both on the same page about the next step in our part of the investigation. I guess what they said about couples thinking alike was true, after all.

Patty, however, was frowning at us. "Mrs. Parsons? Didn't she alibi out?"

Trevor shrugged. "We never followed through to verify that, because it didn't turn out to be murder on that case. Now that there is a murder involved, things are different."

I tried, unsuccessfully, to stifle another yawn. As much as I wanted my nice, soft bed, we needed to keep Patty fully abreast of our thinking processes. That went doubly so now that she was officially back on the case. Or cases, as the case may be.

"A lot different," I said. "I mean, think about it. Say you are a married woman having an illicit love affair with a married man. And then, just suppose, that man has a heart attack and dies while the two of you are, well, taking part in affair-like activities. Who are you going to call for help?"

Patty's eyebrows soared. "You really think she'd call the wife?"

I shrugged, giving her a minute to think about it. She did. I could see the idea slowly forming in her head, even as she talked it out.

"She wouldn't want a big public splash with everyone knowing that she'd been with Parsons at the time of his death," she said slowly. Then she nodded. "And the only one with possibly even more to lose than herself in that situation would be Parsons' own wife."

Patty looked me in the eye. "It was all about saving their reputations, wasn't it?"

"That would be my guess, yes," I said. The next yawn required a stretch, telling me things were progressing, and that I really needed to be getting to bed before things with my body and mind went south.

Besides, Destiny was likely waiting for me at home, too. It didn't do for me to be too late for that nightly trip to the Ether to dump some of my magical overload. That was especially true when I was in the middle of a case. And even more so if that case involved someone I truly cared about.

And I cared about Patty. Somewhere along the line, the woman had become family.

And family was everything to a Ravenswind.

The next morning, I felt on top of the world. Destiny, however, looked a little more drained than usual.

"In the future, let's try to make time to dump at least a little magic during the day, all right?" She suggested. "Last night just about did me in. You might have had a restful sleep. I, however, had to pull a double shift. You know cats sleep a lot during the night, too, right?"

"That bad, huh?"

She nodded.

"Sorry." I hesitated. "Things are a bit crazy right now, but I promise I'll try to take time out to dump a little magic here and there where I can. And when things even out, I'll try to work it into a new routine. Okay?"

Destiny sniffed. "I'd ask you to do more than try, but I guess that's a start. Just know that the Ether isn't a simple place to navigate. If I were to, oh, say fall asleep while I had your soul there, things could get really ugly, really fast."

I gulped. I'd never thought about that. Okay, so maybe I'd do more than just try. I mean, it wasn't like there weren't opportunities abounding all around me that I could spend a little magic on. Timing and secrecy were more the issues at hand.

But for something that important, I'd just have to make the effort, now wouldn't I?

Trevor came out of the bathroom. "Shower's all yours, and I left you plenty of hot water. You're welcome."

After a nice hot shower, albeit a short one—Trevor hadn't been so right about that plenty of hot water thing—I bounced back to that top of the world feeling again. We so had a handle on this thing.

I wasn't sure how the deputy sheriff tied in with Mrs. Parsons, but I was pretty certain that we could figure it all out in the end. With any luck, by sunset today, we'd have the killer—or killers, as the case may be—all locked up in a nice little jail cell.

Patty could go back to being sheriff, and the remaining commissioners could issue a heartfelt apology to her for putting her through all this. And then beg her to stay sheriff.

I was banking on that last part, by the way. If they had brains in those heads of theirs, that would happen. If it didn't? Well, then it would be time to get the community involved.

We could do that, too.

We had decided against calling ahead to let Mrs. Parsons know we were coming. When you called ahead, you gave the person an opportunity to say no. Just showing up at their front doorstep limited their ability to do that.

That was an important thing to remember when you were a private investigator. After all, we couldn't arrest someone for refusing to talk to us. If they didn't talk, there wasn't much we could do, legally, to make them.

Having Trevor with me helped. A lot. Everyone knew that not only was he a sheriff's deputy, he was also Orville Taylor's son. Granted, he was currently an off-duty sheriff's deputy, but then we weren't exactly going to lead with that information, were we?

Yes. It might have been a slight shade of a gray area. Murder, however, was a most definite shade of black. I rather thought using a little gray to catch a black was worth it. And it wasn't like we were flashing the woman his badge. We just weren't mentioning the whole honeymoon slash vacation thing.

When the door opened and I got a look at her expression upon seeing us standing there, I thought it was a very good thing we hadn't called ahead. To say she wasn't happy to see us would be an understatement. A vast one, at that.

"What do you two want?"

"Ten minutes of your time?" Trevor said with a smile. That man could charm just about anyone with that smile of his. Apparently, Mrs. Parsons was just as susceptible as most women were to it. Kind of worrying to me at times, that powerful smile of his.

She hesitated but finally opened the door wide enough to allow us in. Then she led us into the living room. Or the parlor, as she would probably call it. It was a heck of a lot fancier than our old-fashioned living room. I didn't really think her family did much living in that room.

Sad, really.

"I suppose this is about Johnny's death?" she asked. "But then, if it is, I don't really understand what you are here for. The coroner is a friend of mine. I know now that Johnny's death was by heart attack. No murder involved at all."

"I wouldn't be so quick to say that," Trevor said slowly. "And there are other crimes involved in all this, too. Crimes like moving a body to incriminate someone else. That kind of thing is pretty serious on its own."

She was frowning at him. Whether she'd heard his whole comment or not was up for debate. She seemed pretty focused on that first part.

"What do you mean you wouldn't be so quick to say it wasn't murder? The coroner knows more about that than you do, surely. If he says Johnny died of natural causes, then he did, right?"

"Your husband died of a heart attack, yes. But unfortunately, that isn't where this crime spree ended."

She swallowed. "It isn't?"

Huh. What do you know? Orville must have done a bang-up job keeping the news of finding Glenda's body away from the local news channels. That was pretty dang impressive.

"No. It isn't. Glenda Klein's body was found yesterday. The all-knowing coroner puts her time of death very close to that of your husbands." He paused. "Heck of a coincidence, that is. Don't you think?"

She turned away. Yeah. A person could only hold an act in place for so long. She knew a heck of a lot more than she'd told us thus far. If she wasn't the killer, then she dang well knew who was. I'd bet a lot on that.

When she turned back to us, her face was that of a statue. Not a single emotion showing. "I'm going to go out on a limb and say that you two know Johnny was having an affair with the woman."

"We do," I said. "And we also know that he and Glenda had been to see a divorce attorney. The very day he died, in fact. But then, you knew that, didn't you?" I was getting rather tired of her dancing around the fact. Better to get things out into the open, I thought, and then go from there.

Her head raised a fraction of an inch. "I'm guessing Mr. Klein told you I called him with that news, so I will not deny it. My cousin works in that attorney's office." She grimaced. "A fact that Johnny seems to have forgotten in the heat of the moment." She sighed as she sat down. "But you should know that this isn't the first time Johnny has done this kind of thing. He never goes through with it. It's his way of convincing his current affair that he's serious about her. Nothing was filed with the courts. It never is."

Okay, so that was a new angle on things. One that would be worth checking out. Right now, though, I didn't think it meant all that much. It was entirely possible that this time was different with good old Johnny. And it was also entirely possible that Mrs. Parsons had known that, too.

She shook her head and squeezed a tiny tear out of her right eye. I'd always been envious of women who could cry on demand.

"I'd never have called him if I'd known he'd go this far. I bet Johnny had that heart attack when he showed up and caught them together. But to kill his own wife? I hope you've made an arrest?"

Ah, so that was her game. It made a lot of sense, now that I thought about it. In fact, it made so much sense that I had yet another question for Mr. Klein. I wanted to know exactly when the woman had made that knowledge-sharing phone call.

Before or after Parsons had died?

Chapter 20

We'd barely made it outside the Parsons' front door when my cell phone started blaring. I glanced at it before answering. Ruby. I really hoped she wasn't calling to ask for my help with her latest bond take-down. My plate was a little too full at the moment.

"Hey, Ruby. How's it going?"

"Where are you?"

Okay, so now I was frowning. This wasn't a normal social call. Not with all the worry and stress in Ruby's voice.

"Trevor and I are in Wind's Crossing. What's wrong?"

"Get home. As soon as possible. Patty's wards are going off, and I don't know how to deactivate them. I cast a soundproof spell on the bathroom to make this call, but her wards are already starting to eat right through it."

She wasn't kidding either, as I could hear a high-pitched squeal building over the phone. I motioned to Trevor, and the two of us were already running toward our car. "Have you called Patty?"

"Yeah, but it went straight to voice mail. Just get here already, okay? Do you think our wards are loud? Wait until you hear Patty's."

I kind of already could. In person? They had to be downright deafening.

"We're on our way."

I don't know if Trevor was relying on the Wind's Crossing police knowing his vehicle or just trusting to luck, but we made the drive in record time. He wasn't generally one to break the law. Any law. Even that of keeping to the posted speed limit.

Today, he made an exception. I truly don't think I could have beaten his time, even on a broom. If I'd had a broom at hand.

I didn't, or I would have been tempted to try. As I said, there was far too much stress and worry in Ruby's voice for me to be lolly-gagging around here.

A mile from the estate, we could hear a high-pitched, extremely annoying sound in the far distance. Trevor's eyes widened as he glanced over at me.

"Surely that isn't...?" he asked.

But it was. The noise grew louder the closer we got to home. By the time we pulled into our driveway, I was worried about permanent hearing damage if it went on much longer.

Lucky for us, Orville's patrol car wheeled into the driveway behind us, and the sound just... stopped. Like someone flipped a switch. Which is probably exactly what happened. Patty threw her magical switch as she stepped out of Orville's car and ran toward her cabin.

By unanimous agreement, we all let her lead. Well, that and the fact that I really don't think any of us would be up to beating Patty in a foot race. That woman was speed incarnate. Especially in times when speed mattered.

The cabin looked the same on the outside, and Patty went in, hair flying with unused magical discharge, and came out a second later. "The house is okay. You can come in if you want."

We did. With the size of her house, and that many people, there wasn't a lot of room to move around. But a quick glance showed me that everything looked the same as it had the last time I'd been there.

It was pretty apparent to me that Patty's wards had done the trick. Whoever had been here snooping around and up to no good had been scared off when the high-pitched alarms had gone off. Not to mention the fact that they would have had to leave pretty darn quickly if they'd wanted to preserve their ability to hear.

I stepped back outside in time to see Destiny and Jesse barreling toward the tiny cabin. At Destiny's insistence, coupled with the fact that we'd been pretty sure we'd be gone no more than a couple of hours, we'd left our newest family member in her care.

It was probably best to find out now just how little good our new fence was going to be at actually keeping Jesse in the yard. At this point, it was probably more for show than anything, as I was positive that I'd locked that blasted gate behind me this morning.

Then again, if there was a way to get through a locked gate, my Destiny would surely know it. And the Goddess got what the Goddess wanted. That was just a fact of nature.

Destiny only took a second once they reached me to catch her breath before mentally shouting her urgent news. "Athena is gone!"

My heart dropped as my eyes flew down to meet her terrified gaze. "What do you mean Athena is gone?"

In a heartbeat, Patty was standing by my side, her eyes on Destiny as well. "Did they take her?"

It wasn't me she was asking, but as I'd have to act as an interpreter in this situation, it all amounted to the same. I waited for Destiny's answer.

I really didn't like her hesitation.

"I can't say that for positive. But I think maybe they did. I know she was here this morning, and after the wards broke loose with all the ruckus, Jesse kind of freaked. It took me a few minutes to calm her down and help dampen the noise a bit for her. That had to be hard on a dog's ears."

After I relayed her words to Patty, the woman just blinked at me. "And after that?" she asked.

"Once I got Jesse calmed down, I sent out a feeler for Athena to check on her. That's when I realized she was missing."

Patty nodded grimly and went back into the cabin, only to emerge a second later with a Find spell in her hand. No, the bag wasn't labeled, but I've seen enough Find spells in my day to know one when I saw one. Plus, that spell was the one we needed at the moment.

She didn't hesitate to cast the spell, and the thin blue line appeared before us. And wouldn't you know it, the line followed the trail of tire tracks the jerk had left in Patty's freshly mowed yard.

Just like that, we were all on the move again. Only this time, not all of us were in cars.

Patty had headed for Orville's squad car. That made sense, as he had the lights and sirens to give us the ability to speed to our heart's content. But Ruby had stopped her mid-way.

"I think this calls for brooms over wheels."

Patty swallowed, then looked at me. "I've never flown a broom."

"You can ride with me," I told her. "But for once, I think Ruby is right. Orville's squad car will give them speed, but they will still have to follow the roads. On brooms, roads aren't an issue."

Her hesitation didn't even last a full second. "So be it. Let's get the brooms."

"Um, I hate to say this," Trevor said. "I understand what you are saying, but we're going to need one of you, at least, in the vehicle with us. We can't see that magic line, remember?"

Ruby was wavering. I could tell she hated to waste the opportunity to ride her broom. And the whole thing had been her idea, too. The problem was, she wasn't strong enough to take on a passenger. I was.

And unfortunately, Arc was at the law firm. It was only the three of us.

"Fine," Ruby said. "I'll go with the men, and we'll meet you there."

Then she gave me a look. She didn't say it, but I got the meaning all too well. I'd owe her a nice long broom ride. Soon, too.

The fact that Patty and I had to run to my house to pick up my heavy-duty broom gave the others a small head start. A head start that was only slightly mitigated by the insistence of Destiny and Jesse on tagging along.

I glanced back to see them jumping into the back seat with Trevor. I'd kind of figured their joint willpower would win out. My familiar was nothing if not persuasive. And heaven help us once Jesse became a familiar too. We humans just might not stand a chance.

All I could do was hope that whoever had taken Athena had the brains not to harm one little strand of fur on that feline's body. If they did, then they'd better dang well be praying for heaven to help them. Because the Goddess sure as heck wouldn't.

And neither would we.

CHAPTER 21

I had vastly underestimated Orville's ability to get the speed he needed. With Ruby guiding their way, by the time Patty and I landed, we could already hear the siren headed our way.

Sounded close, too. I was just about to suggest to Patty that it might behoove us to wait for our backup. And I would have done just that, too. If I could have caught up with her before she made it to the Parsons' front door.

That's right. We were right back at the Parsons' house. Only there was another vehicle in the driveway now. An Oak Hill Deputy's vehicle at that.

The sight of that SUV sitting there had me really wishing I'd caught up to Patty in time. I thought having Orville in on this would be a very good thing. But it wasn't going to happen in time.

Patty's closed fist made contact with the door so hard the wood shook. There was a bit of magic behind those blows. And yes, her hair was flying. Unfortunately, a quick side glance showed my hair doing the same.

Dang all this pent-up magic, anyway. I'd have to be very careful in the next few minutes. I'd also need to hunt out an opportunity to safely discharge some of that energy soon. If I didn't, all kinds of bad things could happen.

I would have thought the broom ride would have helped. But apparently the levitation spell had invited the area magic to come along for the ride. And it had accepted, too.

Mrs. Parsons put the chain on the door before opening it. That meant that most likely she'd already looked out to see who was standing there. She stared at us through the three-inch gap between the door and the doorframe.

"I'm not talking with you. You aren't the sheriff right now, and I don't have to." She went to close the door, but Patty blocked it.

Hard.

"I'm not here to talk," Patty growled. Wolves seemed to have the ability to actually growl words. Who knew? "I'm here to collect my cat."

Lisa blinked at her. "Your cat?"

The woman could have won an Oscar for that performance. If I hadn't just taken a broom ride following a line of magic straight to her front door, I'd have been a lot more apt to believe that she didn't know what the heck Patty was talking about.

"My cat and my familiar," Patty said, still with more than a little growl to it. And yes, the growl was making Mrs. Parsons decidedly uncomfortable. It would me, too, if it had been directed at me.

"Why on earth would you think your cat was here?"

The sound of tires on gravel behind us told me our backup had arrived. Looked like maybe Orville made it in time, after all. If only Patty could contain herself for a few more precious seconds.

Unfortunately, Patty was at the end of her rope. Not that I could blame her. If Destiny had been in that house, I'd have taken the door down too. Probably with a lot more force than Patty used. As it was, she only tore the chain mechanism off the frame.

If it had been me, they would have had to replace the whole dang door.

The problem was that once the door opened, without Mrs. Parsons' consent, we found ourselves staring down the short barrel of a Smith and Wesson revolver. Held by a man in a brown deputy uniform.

With the hatred shining in his eyes, I had no doubt that he was about to pull the trigger. And the law would probably back him up too. After all, a non-law-enforcement person had just broken into the house.

I grabbed Patty's arm and jerked her to the side, just as the bullet flew past where she'd been standing. We hit the deck of the porch just as Orville took the porch steps in one giant leap.

His gun was drawn, too. And pointed at the other man in uniform.

"Lower your weapon now," Orville said. There wasn't an ounce of growl in his voice. However, that didn't make it one little bit less scary.

The other man was a deputy, yes, and in full uniform, to boot. But Orville was wearing a sheriff's badge, and we were right smack dab in the center of his jurisdiction, too. The deputy had to know that didn't bode well for him.

He tried out a smile with a curt nod to Orville. "Holstering it now, sir. You saw those women forcing their way in, didn't you?" He nodded to the broken remains of the chain, now hanging loosely from the door. "I had a right to protect property against invasion." The man squared his shoulders. "It's in the constitution."

Even when the revolver was back in the holster, Orville's gun remained out and free. And still pointed at the deputy, too.

"Very slowly, I want you to unbuckle your gun belt and place it on the floor. Then I want your hands on top of your head. Is that understood?"

The man bristled. "What right do you have to ask that? I've done nothing wrong here."

"My request stands." Orville wasn't one to argue. That didn't mean he didn't get his way.

Of course, it probably helped that my Trevor was standing there right beside Orville, backing him up all the way. Trevor, being on vacation, wasn't in uniform, nor did he have a firearm. None of that mattered.

What mattered was what Trevor did have. A very big, and very tense, German Shepherd on a very short and very taut leash.

Yup. Jesse was going to fit in with our team just fine. She wasn't exactly straining at the end of the leash, but at the same time, you could tell that all it would take would be a single word from Trevor and the deputy would be down.

In fact, as the deputy lowered his gun belt to the ground, his eyes were on Jesse more than they were on Orville and his gun. Mine probably would have been too. Guns didn't really show their intent.

Jesse was showing hers in full view of everyone there.

Orville had the pair step out onto the porch with all of us. Good call, that. Who knows what kind of weapons might be hidden in that house? Out in the open was just a safer option for all concerned.

Trevor held a hand down to me. Oh yeah, guess Patty and I should stand up now, shouldn't we?

Mrs. Parsons was glaring at the man by her side. "What have you done now?"

His head snapped around to look at her. "Don't say another word. I haven't done anything."

Patty was about to go off again, I could tell, but just then Destiny gave an extremely loud meow. Much louder, in fact, than any normal cat could manage. There was more than a little magic in that yowl of hers. And the funny thing was, that magic hadn't gone through me.

Huh. Guess Destiny had some magic all of her own. Good to know.

I elbowed Patty and motioned toward Destiny. She was sitting on top of the deputy's squad car. "I'm betting you'll find Athena in that vehicle."

Sparing a glance at Mrs. Parsons, I lucked into seeing her glare at the deputy. That glare must have been the final straw.

"I didn't take any stupid cat. Why on earth would I do that?"

And yet, there was Athena, standing on her tiny little back feet, front feet braced on the passenger side window of the backseat. Her little mouth was opening and closing, but no sound was making it out from the vehicle. Squad cars did a pretty good job of keeping the noise inside where it belonged.

In most cases, anyway.

The man stared at the cat, blinking rapidly. "How the heck did she get in there?" Then his expression changed as he glared at Patty. "You put her there! This is a frame-up."

"Actually, he didn't take Athena," Destiny told me. "She hitched a ride. I guess she thought that would be the only way of leading us to the person who was trying to break in at Patty's." Destiny looked rather thoughtful. "Kind of wish I'd thought of that. Could come in useful in the future."

Oh Goddess, no. Destiny already had a habit of hitching rides she shouldn't be hitching. I really didn't want that to increase. The feline was likely to get herself into something she couldn't get out of. Magic of her own or no.

As Patty was no longer forcing the issue, I had to assume that Athena was telling her pretty much the same thing. But that didn't stop her from walking over to the vehicle in question. The doors were locked.

She glanced back at the deputy. He swallowed, then looked at Orville. "I didn't take that cat, and I'd be more than happy to unlock the doors, but I have to reach into my pocket for the keys."

Orville nodded, and within seconds, Athena was in Patty's arms. Right where she belonged. Which brought up a good point.

Destiny was still on the roof of the vehicle, but more on the driver's side of the car. I had to walk around the entire vehicle to reach her. When I saw the driver's door, I had to wonder if that little forced stroll had been intentional on Destiny's part.

Because that door was riddled with scratch marks. Marks just like what an angry and frustrated dog might make.

CHAPTER 22

I looked over the car at the group on the porch. "I think I'd like to know how you got these scratches on your car door."

Mrs. Parsons was back to glaring at the man. Well, she'd never really stopped, to be honest, but the glare was definitely heating up. If I put a little pressure on... the woman just might break.

The deputy must have thought the same thing. "Seriously, Lisa, don't say a single word."

Orville had finally holstered his gun. Not that it meant a lot in the long run. Orville, wearing his badge, was a scary man. With or without a gun drawn. But with Jesse backing him up? Yeah, if I was the couple on the porch, I'd be pretty dang worried right about now.

Especially as Orville narrowed his eyes at them. "I'd like an answer to Amie's question. How did you get scratches on your vehicle's door?"

You could almost see the wheels turning in the man's mind. Finally, he broke. At least, kind of. I mean, there wasn't much use in denying that a canine had made the marks. That could be too easily proved, couldn't it?

"They happened during an arrest I made a few days back. There was a dog that didn't take kindly to the arrest of its owner. It's in my incident report."

"And the date of that report?" Orville's voice still held not an ounce of emotion. If the man had known him at all, he'd have known just how much trouble he was in.

The man swallowed and tried to take a stand. "I think I have a right to know exactly what you're implying with this line of questioning. I have done nothing wrong here. And I did not take that cat."

Orville glanced back at Patty, and she gave a quick nod. "It's possible that she jumped into the vehicle when he was setting off the wards at my place." Then the man had another pair of serious eyes staring at him. "I won't press cat-napping charges, but I want to know what you doing messing around my property. And you should know, those wards you set off wouldn't have gone off if you'd been pure of heart."

The man snorted. Honest to Goddess snorted. "I don't buy into that magic stuff, so save your breath." Then he looked at Athena with a frown. It wasn't like he could deny being there, now was it? "I was there to ask you some questions about the night Parsons' body was found. When the alarms started going off and you didn't stop them, I had to assume you weren't home. So I left."

"And came straight here," Orville said. "I find that rather odd. In fact, I find a lot of things odd at the moment. So odd that I think I'll make a quick phone call while we're all standing here. If you don't want to answer my question, I'm pretty sure your boss will."

Mrs. Parsons made a move to distance herself from the deputy—we really had to get the man's name sooner or later—but he saw her move for what it was and grabbed her. One arm snaked around the woman's neck, holding her in front of him, even as his other arm reached behind him to pull yet another firearm from the back of his waistband. No revolver this time. The weapon had more than enough bullets to end us all and still have some to spare.

Orville's hand was on his gun, but he didn't have time to draw it. None of us really had the time to react. It happened just that fast.

Only, one of us wasn't going by human instinct. One of us was powered by sheer animal motivation.

Even as the man swung the weapon around to point toward Orville—the biggest threat in the man's eyes—Jesse sprang into action.

The gun went off, but the shot, thankfully, went wild. After that, the weapon dropped onto the porch, where Trevor snatched it up in a heartbeat.

I guess I should note here that the firearm wasn't the only thing that hit the floor of that porch. It was a three-body jumble, but the important thing was that Jesse was on top. And most definitely in charge.

Silly me thought that at that point, the main point of danger had passed. Then I got a look at Trevor's eyes as he looked over at me.

It took that for me to stop and realize that my entire body was tingling with unspent magic. The magic had sensed the danger and had come to help. Only, well, now there was nowhere for it to safely go.

Destiny yowled in my arms. "Get out of sight, fast, so you can dump some of this before we both explode!"

And no, she wasn't exaggerating. Not one tiny bit.

We headed around the side of the house at a dead run. Lucky for us, the Parsons lived on the very outskirts of town, so there weren't any close neighbors that I had to worry about seeing what was about to happen.

My eyes scanned the large backyard for something to dump magic into. There wasn't time for a slow drain into the ground. Not as far and as quickly as this had come.

Every hair on my body was standing at attention with a magical charge that was oh so much more potent than simple electricity. I was a walking, talking, ticking time bomb for sure.

"Pull out an emergency acorn!" Destiny screamed.

Thank the Goddess for my clear-headed feline. The magic was making it hard to think. I swung my small pack around to the front and dug in the side pocket for the small bag of acorns I carried everywhere. It had been Destiny's idea.

One of her better ones, I had to say. Pulling out a single acorn, I pushed it into the dirt as far as I could, then took one last look around to be sure we were in the clear. No one in sight.

I stepped back a few feet from the newly planted acorn and put my hands and the ground. Then I just... let it go.

The result was instant and extremely dramatic. Where there had been bare grass not five minutes before now stood a tall, sturdy oak tree. I swallowed as I looked up at it.

Then I did what I normally did in these situations.

I passed out.

Chapter 23

I came to a few minutes later to find Destiny curled up asleep on my chest, and my cousin Ruby sitting calmly at my side. We'd been through this kind of thing too many times for her to be too worried about me. By now, she knew the pattern of these episodes as well as I did.

Following her eyes, I stared up at the huge tree towering over us.

"That oak tree is kinda new, isn't it?" Ruby asked.

I nodded.

"Emergency acorn, huh?"

Another nod from me. It would take me another minute or two to actually be capable of speech. Handling that amount of magic does things to a witch. Believe me.

As this wasn't Ruby's first rodeo, as they say, she just started doing the talking for me. I appreciated that.

"Jesse really saved the day back there, you know. I think you guys got a winner there."

She wasn't the only one that thought that. If any of us had been holding out on the intelligence of our decision, I didn't think they would be anymore.

"Orville, Patty, and Trevor are escorting Mrs. Parsons and Deputy Mills to the station now. The wife confessed. Well, more like she pinned the whole thing on Mills. But I think it will all come out soon enough. Seems the two of them had been an item for a while. Parsons' wife thought that if they could get Patty out of the way, Mills might stand a chance to win the next sheriff's election."

Made sense. The woman didn't strike me as the type to settle for a mere deputy. But a sheriff? Yeah, being the wife of the sheriff held every bit as much prestige as being the wife of a county commissioner.

Maybe even more. I mean, there was only one sheriff, right?

She must have seen that I still had questions because she took pity on me. "Let's see, what else? Oh, yeah, Glenda Klein, right?"

I gave a weak nod.

Ruby leaned back and took a deep breath. "Well, not surprisingly, that's where Deputy Mills had grave issues with Mrs. Parsons' version of what happened. According to him, Lisa went a little nuts seeing her husband in the, well, state that they found him in and went for Glenda. Supposedly, it was an accident. Her head just happened to make contact with the sharp edge of the lamp on the corner of Parsons' desk when she fell back."

I managed to raise an eyebrow.

"Yeah, I don't think any of us are buying that story, but they've confessed to at least a hand in her death. It'll be up to the prosecuting attorney to get the story straight. You all caught the bad guys... your job is done."

She had a point.

Then it hit me. We'd only had the one vehicle here. If Trevor, Patty, and Orville had went to the station, then where did that leave us? Sure, they'd probably called for another deputy to come to make the transport less crowded and to separate the two, but still... I didn't think Orville would have left his squad car behind.

"They coming back for us?" My voice didn't have a lot of power behind it, but at least I got it loud enough for her to hear my question.

Ruby blushed. "Well, I didn't know the extreme nature of the situation before I sent them on their way. So no."

"Broom?"

Her blush deepened, and she nodded. "Of course, that was before I realized that you'd grown another bloody oak tree. There probably isn't enough power in you right now to get the thing off the ground, is there?"

I shook my head. "Sorry." Then I reached up slowly—believe me when I say slow was the best I could do—to tap the power amulet around her neck.

She grinned at me. "You think it's enough to get us home?"

My hand went from her amulet to the center of my chest, where mine rested under my shirt.

Her grin grew. "If I draw from the amulets... do you think I can drive?"

My smile was a lot weaker than her outright grin. "I kind of think you're gonna have to." Then another thought hit me. Riding a broom, even as a passenger, rather required one to be in a sitting position. And I wasn't quite there just yet. "Give me another few minutes?"

Ruby gave me a hard look. "Are you okay?"

"I will be. Just... a tiny little nap sounds really good right now. You mind?"

She must have realized at that point that the only movement I'd made so far had been the two very slow arm gestures. Her eyes narrowed at me.

I yawned. "Truly, I'll be fine. I'm just really tired right now. Give me half an hour, and I'll be able to ride home with you."

Destiny raised her head to stare into my eyes. "Make that an hour, and you might be of more help on the ride home if she gets into trouble. I can feed you a trickle of magic while you sleep."

I swallowed. My familiar had a good point. I relayed her message to Ruby.

She looked from me to Destiny, then gave a quick nod. "If that's what it takes, then get to sleep already."

Like I had much choice at that point. I was already dozing off. Part of me thought just maybe Destiny had a little something to do with that.

The next morning, I felt a whole lot better. About everything. With the clearing of Patty's name in full, plus the added little detail that it had been Parsons' wife that had set her up, the other commissioners had canceled the competency hearing. They'd even gone a step farther and issued a formal apology to her.

She had more than deserved that.

So now, things were pretty much back to normal. Just the way I liked them. Sure, Trevor and I had missed the opportunity for a true honeymoon, but that was more than okay. We had the rest of our lives to make up for that. I kind of hoped the honeymoon was only just beginning for us.

All that wonderful peace and happiness lasted until Trevor rolled over to gaze wonderingly into my eyes. I smiled at him. I mean, we were still newlyweds, after all.

But an early statement of love wasn't what was on his mind.

"How far along in the witch's journey do I need to be before I can make Jesse my familiar?"

I thought about it. "There aren't actually any written rules about that. It's up to the individual witch. Some prefer to come into their power a bit before choosing a familiar and making it official. Others take their familiar first and then work with them for the whole journey."

"So a neophyte can take a familiar? I don't have to make it to level one?"

I kind of thought I knew where this was going. And what that meant for the day ahead.

"They can."

He took a deep breath. "Will you help me, then? I want to do this sooner rather than later." Then he paused with a glance over at Destiny. His next words came slowly, as if he was feeling them out as he said them. "She can talk to Yorkie, can't she?"

Destiny returned his glance and cocked her head at him. In times like this, I wished I wasn't the only one she could communicate with. Well, the only human she could communicate with. It was tiring being the interpreter all the time.

Only, right now she wasn't saying anything. Just staring at Trevor.

I sighed. My cat could be so anal about things sometimes. "I think she wants you to ask her that question instead of me."

He blinked at me for a minute. "Oh." Then he turned back to the cat sitting on the dresser. "Sorry about that, Destiny. Can you talk to Yorkie? No, scratch that. What I really want to know is... can you talk to Jesse? I'd kind of like to know if she would be all right with becoming a familiar."

Destiny was hesitating. We waited.

"I can communicate with Yorkie and Athena just fine. And some other animals too." Her head turned away slightly. "But the other animal has to be open to it. Jesse has been through something really, really bad. I can tell. She isn't open to communication just yet." She perked up. "But I will say that the communication becomes much easier and stronger between two familiars. Once she's your familiar, I should be able to read her fairly well." She wrinkled her nose slightly. "Even if you are just a neophyte hedge witch."

I relayed her message word for word. If she'd meant that last part as an insult, Trevor didn't seem to take it that way. He was too happy to hear about the first part. And truthfully, she'd said nothing more than the truth. Calling a rose anything other than a rose doesn't make the rose change, does it?

After a moment of silence, I looked at him. "So, are you wanting to do the spell and make it official?"

He took a deep breath, still staring at Destiny. "Destiny, one more question, if I may. Do you think Jesse would be okay with becoming my familiar?"

She considered for a long minute, then slowly inclined her head. "I can tell she adores you. And becoming a familiar only makes the bond stronger."

She paused to lick her paw and rub her ear. I knew that as a timeout to gather her thoughts. Finally, she looked back at him. "To be honest, I think the sooner you make Jesse your familiar the better. It might help with her anxiety a little. With that tight of a bond, maybe she'll stop worrying about being left behind again." Another brief pause. "Or whatever else she's worrying about."

"Thank you. That helps a lot." Then Trevor turned to me. "Let's do this."

Epilogue (Destiny and the Familiars)

The humans ran around all day long, getting things ready. Gathering fresh ingredients for the spell—taking a familiar was slightly different for a hedge witch versus an elemental—and researching the best way to go about it.

In the end, they just called in one of the hedge witches on our team, Lily Hilton. She put them straight in no time flat. Even went so far as to give them the spell she'd used to take her familiar. Of course, that spell came with a warning that it should be changed to fit the need in Trevor's case.

Writing a spell to take a familiar was rather like writing your own wedding vows, I thought. They were very personal to the witch in question. The more personal, the better actually. It helped to create that solid bond between the two souls.

I glanced up at the heavens. The night was clear, at least. That part was good. A full moon would have been better, of course, but that would have required waiting. No one wanted that.

The other familiars and I were waiting under the big oak tree on the hilltop behind the old farmhouse for the humans to be ready. They were taking their own sweet time about it.

Jesse was getting agitated by the waiting, I could tell. She had to know something important was about to happen. But she wasn't able to comprehend the significance of the humans' actions.

I just hoped I hadn't been wrong when I said that her becoming a familiar would help us communicate. Either way, we'd all know by the end of the night, wouldn't we?

Yorkie nudged Jesse. "Bend down," he said. Jesse just looked at him, then over at me. Like I could interpret for her. But maybe I could at that.

I laid down on the ground and looked up at her. She wasn't a dumb dog. Far from it. She got my meaning straight away. Shoot, another few days, and I might not have needed the familiar spell to open the communication doors.

Jesse was warming to our little family's way of life.

The big dog laid down next to me, giving Yorkie the ability to groom the stray fur on the top of Jesse's head.

"You want to look your best for this," Yorkie told her.

Hmm. Yorkie had a point. The spell would act a lot faster if Jesse were relaxed, too. And there wasn't anything much more relaxing than a gentle back massage.

I climbed up on Jesse's back and started pit-patting. And purring. Music to help the body reach a gentle flow state, purring was. It worked too.

Between me and Yorkie, we had Jesse all relaxed—and looking her best—by the time the humans were ready. If they did a slight double-take when they looked over and saw us helping Jesse prepare? Well, that was just the icing on the cake.

They tended to underestimate us sometimes. Okay, more often than not, actually.

Trevor called Jesse to him, and Yorkie and I followed the dog over. The show was about to start. Finally.

The neophyte witch and his soon-to-be familiar settled down in the very center of the clearing. Funny how, with both of them sitting face to face like that, their eyes were pretty much on an equal level. Jesse was not a small canine.

Trevor reached out and gently placed his hands on Jesse's paws. The dog cocked her head, but sat there still as stone, waiting for whatever came next.

With a quick throat clearing, the neophyte stared deeply into Jesse's eyes.

Witch and familiar, till Death do we part
A chance for each, our lives to restart
I shall be yours, and you shall be mine
Forever and ever, our souls shall twine
This decision is made freely by me
With that said, so mote it be.

I was a mere kitten when I'd become my witch's familiar, but even so, I think I would have remembered glowing when she spoke those final words. I'm not at all sure that I had.

Jesse, however, did.

The canine was sitting up even straighter—if that were possible—still staring into her witch's eyes.

"Does this mean... I'm family?" Her voice, if you can call it a voice, was low and unsure. But oh so full of hope that it just about broke my heart.

Yorkie and I stepped up to either side of her, and I laid a paw on top of Trevor's hand, which was still on top of Jesse's paw. Yorkie laid his paw on top of mine.

I did my best to give her a smile and sent a strong purr to back it up.

"Silly dog, you've been family from the first day they brought you home," I told her. "But now, you're even better."

"You're a familiar."

###